School
of
Charm

School
of
Charm

LISA ANN SCOTT

KATHERINE TEGEN BOOKS
An Imprint of HarperCollins Publishers

Katherine Tegen Books is an imprint of HarperCollins Publishers.

School of Charm
Copyright © 2014 by Lisa Ann Scott

Library of Congress Cataloging-in-Publication Data
Scott, Lisa Ann.
  School of Charm / Lisa Ann Scott. — First edition.
    pages cm
  Summary: After her beloved father's death in 1977, eleven-year-old tomboy
Chip tries to fit with her family of beauty queens, making unlikely new
friends at Miss Vernie's unusual charm school in Mt. Airy, North Carolina.
  ISBN 978-0-06-220758-6 (hardcover bdg.)
  [1. Individuality—Fiction. 2. Self-perception—Fiction. 3. Family life—
North Carolina—Fiction. 4. Beauty contests—Fiction. 5. Tomboys—Fiction.
6. Race relations—Fiction. 7. North Carolina—History—20th century—
Fiction.] I. Title.
PZ7.S42673Sch 2014   2013014341
[Fic]—dc23   CIP
                                                              AC

Typography by Joel Tippie
14 15 16 17 18   CG/RRDH   10 9 8 7 6 5 4 3 2 1
❖
First Edition

To my father, David Eder,
who died when I was four.
And to my second father, Tim Scott,
who took over the role when David could not.
I love you both.

School
of
Charm

chapter one

"TELL ME AGAIN WHY WE HAVE TO MOVE TO Grandma's?" I chewed on my thumb waiting for Mama's answer, but I knew what she was going to say. I was still hoping she'd change her mind, and sometimes nagging helped. Mama said if nagging were an Olympic sport, I'd win a gold medal. But I only did it for important things. And this was the most important thing ever. This changed everything.

Mama's eyes flashed in the rearview mirror. She yanked the steering wheel to the right and pulled over the car. Me, Charlene, and Ruthie slid across the seat, crashing into each other. Our U-Haul trailer rocked to a stop and dust blew up behind it.

Rats. Sometimes nagging ended like this, with Mama madder than a bee in a pop can.

Mama turned off her Elvis cassette and stuck her head between the two front seats. She smiled hard with her mouth but not her eyes, just like in her Miss North Carolina first runner-up picture. Her dark red hair looked like a puffy storm cloud around her face. "Brenda Anderson, *do not* ask me that again. I told you we have to live with Grandma now because we don't have the money to stay in our house." She kept smiling and blinking fast. I knew I was in trouble when Mama called me Brenda. Normally she called me Chip, just like everyone else did.

We sat real quiet in the backseat. Since Mama was already mad and couldn't reach my earlobe to give it a good twist, I decided to get brave. "But we've never even met Grandma. I'm eleven years old, and I've never once gotten a birthday card or a present from her. She didn't even come to Daddy's funeral."

Mama sucked in a big breath and then let it out real slow. "This is our only option, Brenda. Houses don't just pay for themselves. You think I'm thrilled about moving here? I haven't seen Grandma since . . ." But Mama didn't finish her sentence. She turned around, jerked the gearshift, and drove the station wagon back onto the road. She was so close to the car in front of us, it pulled over to let us pass.

"Ow!" I rubbed my arm where my big sister Charlene pinched it.

Charlene glared at me and leaned over. "Quiet, Chip. Don't upset Mama. Don't talk about Daddy," she whispered harshly.

My little sister Ruthie's shoulders curled forward and she shook her head. "I won't talk about him, either. I won't." Her voice came out like a wisp of air.

"Good girl." Charlene kissed her head and Ruthie beamed up at her.

Then Charlene sat forward and patted Mama's shoulder. "Yes, Mama," she said loudly. "We understand. Everything's fine."

I gritted my teeth and crossed my arms. It was not fine. Nothing was.

Mama flipped on her music again and looked back at us. "You're all going to love Mount Airy." She said this all sugary, like she was on a TV commercial and hadn't just been hollering at me. "Did I ever tell you that Mayberry on *The Andy Griffith Show* was modeled after Mount Airy? Of course, that show was a bit before your time, but Mayberry was meant to be the best little town in America. You couldn't ask to live in a nicer place, girls."

Mama had already told us this 837 times. I wanted to ask her if it was so nice, why did she leave and move to New York? But I'd already asked Mama enough questions.

"Yes ma'am," Charlene said. "Mount Airy and North Carolina both sound wonderful."

"'Ma'am'? You already have a southern accent?" I shoved my knees against the seatback and wished I could spit.

Charlene turned on one of those big smiles she'd give ugly boys who whistled at her. "Hush now. I'm a southern belle at heart. Just like Mama. And so are you, baby girl." She tickled Ruthie.

As Ruthie giggled and squirmed to get away, her shiny shoe kicked my shin.

"Agh, Ruthie!" I rubbed my leg.

"Sorry." Then she gave me a great big smile, just like Charlene's, only Ruthie was missing her two front teeth. Soon enough she'd be talking with a drawl too. But not me. I'd pronounce my words fast and flat so people would know I wasn't from the South. And I wouldn't be walking around with that dumb old smile, either.

I leaned against the door and kicked the seat as we drove along. Mama let that Elvis cassette play again and again until I'd heard "Hound Dog" and all the other songs five more times. Ugh. We'd never been in the car for nine whole hours. We drove to the Adirondacks one summer, but that was only six hours away. And Daddy made it fun, singing songs and shouting out faraway states he saw on license plates. "Hello, Arkansas," he'd holler. "Here comes Texas! You're sure far from Florida!"

But this trip wasn't fun at all. I pulled up the door lock. Then I pushed it down. Up and down. Up and down. Faster and faster and faster. Up and down. Up and—

"Brenda!" Mama snapped. "Knock it off. You'll fall out." She stared at me in the mirror for a few seconds. "Hundreds of kids across America tumble out of cars every day doing that very thing. They get swept down the highway and squashed. Flat as a pancake." She smacked her hands together to demonstrate. "You keep that door locked."

I pushed down the lock. Mama was always telling tall tales. But she'd tuck in a few true ones, so you never knew if the one she was telling at the time really happened or not.

I was quiet after that, watching the dirt change colors. My stomach lurched as the roads turned hilly. The tree branches dripped with stringy plants. Mist swirled around their trunks and settled in the dips of the road. This seemed like a spooky kind of place I would not be moving to if I had a say in the whole thing.

My tummy rumbled and I dug out the sandwich I'd stuffed in my pocket. The bologna had turned slimy during our long ride, so I threw it out the window.

"Litterbug," Ruthie said.

"Am not. The birds will eat it." I wasn't sure what was worse: having a big sister or having a little sister. Either way, I felt like the bologna in the middle of my sandwich: stuck, stuck, stuck in this family. And now it was way worse without Daddy.

"Girls!" Mama warned. "This is Grandma's street." She turned down a dusty road and drummed her fingers on the steering wheel. "Now remember, Grandma's not used to the hubbub from you three, so use your best behavior. Chip! Sit up straight, dar-lin'. Your clothes are all wrinkled. Grandma won't like that. She once took scissors and cut a shirt right off my back because I didn't iron it nicely enough." Mama checked herself in the mirror and smacked her lips. She swerved around a rooster strutting in the road.

"Why is Grandma so mean?" I fiddled with the hem of my jean shorts, wondering if she ever cut a pair of pants right off Mama.

Mama let out another long breath. Her mouth made different shapes, searching for the words.

I leaned forward; this was going to be good. Really good.

"Grandma . . . well . . . she . . ." Then Mama deflated just like a balloon does when you quit trying to blow it up. "That's enough questions for today." Her knuckles were white, gripping the steering wheel. "But I'm not kidding. She likes neat and she likes clean."

Charlene flipped her hair over her shoulders. "Oh, she'll love you, Chip." She looked down at my grubby sneakers, then her eyes widened and she screamed. "Mama! Brenda brought that . . . creature with her!" She pressed herself up against the car door.

Mama pulled the car over again. We all went sliding again. We all crashed into each other *again*.

Rats. I picked up the bowl wedged under the seat with the candy wrappers and pop cans.

This time Mama didn't say anything. She blinked at me, waiting.

"I couldn't leave him, Mama."

She closed her eyes and shook her head. "I thought Billy took it when he said good-bye."

"No. He didn't." Billy spent more time hanging

out with me and Daddy than he did at his own house. He hadn't seen his own daddy in years, so I didn't mind sharing mine with Billy. But he hadn't come to our house since Daddy died.

Mama had called Billy's mom to tell her we were moving. He finally showed up early that morning as we were loading the U-Haul. His eyebrows shot right up when he saw that turtle. "Wow. Want me to take care of it?"

I'd pulled the bowl away. "He's coming with me." Between the two of us, this was the best thing we'd ever found. Finally I was winning the Coolest Thing Ever. Not that it mattered. We were moving to North Carolina and Billy wouldn't be my best friend anymore and we wouldn't be playing the Coolest Thing Ever anymore.

"Okay. Bye, Chip." He tucked something in my hand before he ran off.

I looked down and there was the Coolest Thing Ever he had found. The perfectly round rock he'd pulled from the creek. He'd cut open his foot getting that rock. So I felt a little guilty staring at my turtle in the backseat with Mama fuming at me. I should've given him to Billy. Then I wouldn't be in all that trouble. But Billy didn't know why this turtle was so special. Neither did Mama.

Mama shook her head again. "Lordy, Chip. You're taking a big risk bringing that turtle. You'd better get rid of it or hide it real good. Grandma hates animals. She once flushed a fish I won at the church carnival— and it wasn't even dead." Mama looked out the window and then back at me. "And she and Grandpa used to make turtle soup." One red eyebrow popped up.

"Ew! Turtle soup? How gross," Charlene said.

Ruthie pinched her nose and squealed, "How gross!"

Mama pulled back onto the road, and I felt a big lump in my throat. My turtle sloshed around in the water. I found him down by our pond after Daddy's funeral. I'd scooped him up, grabbed one of Mama's cake batter bowls, and ran through the living room packed with mourners. They all stopped talking. But I just slammed my door and sat in my room trying out different names on him: Mickey or Minnie, Jack or Jill. I wasn't even sure if it was a boy or a girl, but I settled on Earl, since he had come early—way early. Turtles are usually laying their eggs around that time—not hatching. That's why finding him was so strange.

I know Daddy would have helped him if he'd been there. So that day, I'd made Daddy a promise up in heaven: I'd take care of that little turtle on my own, even if it meant moving him away from everything he knew and all the way to North Carolina. I set the bowl under the seat so Grandma couldn't see it when we got there. She would not be turning my turtle into soup for dinner. No way.

Mama turned the car into the driveway. She took a deep breath. "Don't screw this up."

I wasn't sure who she was warning.

chapter two

GRANDMA CAME RUNNING OUT IN HIGH HEELS AND A dress, arms waving in the air, pearls swinging. "Good news, girls! I just called, and there's still time to enter the Miss Dogwood pageant. Charlene's fifteen, right? You could be Miss Dogwood 1977!" That was the very first thing Grandma said as we climbed out of the car and lined up to meet her. It was like she'd just seen us yesterday, instead of never knowing us at all.

Grandma looked very pretty for the mean lady from Mama's stories. Loose, red curls of hair framed her face. She had wide, chocolate-brown eyes and a heart-shaped mouth and hardly any wrinkles. I never knew what it was like to have a grandma because Daddy's mother died before I was born. But my idea of a grandma wasn't this lady standing in front of me. She did not look like she was a cookie-baker or a story-reader or a cheek-pincher in her silky dress and long red nails. And her house wasn't like I'd imagined it either. I was expecting some cute cottage tucked into the woods. Her house was very fancy, with big pillars out front.

"Miss Dogwood? Really? Oh my goodness," Charlene said, touching her lips. "You really think I could win, Grandma Cooper?"

I wanted to smack that *Ijustcan'thelpbeingthispretty* look right off her face. I squinted at her instead, sending mean thoughts her way.

Grandma put a hand on her hip. "I was Miss North Carolina 1939. Of course you could win. You've got my looks," Grandma said. "And your mother was first runner-up in 1961. She could have won, too, if she hadn't stumbled during the evening-wear competition."

Mama's eyes hardened like shiny buttons. "Maybe if you'd bought me the shoes I wanted, I wouldn't have fallen."

Grandma sniffed and wagged her finger. "I bought you the best shoes money could buy. And you would have won the next year if you hadn't gone and—"

"Mother," Mama said in her warning voice. She leaned down and brushed off one of my sneakers even though nothing was on it.

Grandma started humming deep in her throat. Then she put on a big smile. Same as Charlene's and Mama's and Ruthie's. Grandma opened her arms. "Oh, welcome home, Cecelia."

Mama did not move to hug her. She nodded, but she didn't smile back. "Mother, this is Charlene and Ruthie." She pushed my sisters forward.

Grandma nodded. "You look like your mama. You've got our red hair!" She worked her hand through Ruthie's curls, dark as a ripe cherry. Then her smile fell. "Who's this one?"

"That's Brenda, Mother."

Grandma's eyes flicked over me. "You look like your father."

No one said anything.

I cleared my throat. "I know. I have the same blond hair, like honey. Same color eyes—blue-green. Did you know he died?" The words just popped out of my mouth, the way a watermelon seed slips between your lips. I couldn't help it.

Grandma squinted down her nose at me as if I was

a bug she was aiming to squash. "Of course I know. Why do you think I'm letting you stay in my home?"

Our eyes locked like we were in a stare-down contest.

Then Mama shot me one of her looks and I stopped. "Sorry, Mother," she said. "We're all tired. It was a long ride." She tucked her hair behind her ears and rubbed her eyes.

Mama did look tired, and not just from the ride. Billy always said I had the prettiest mama in the whole class. I warned him he better not let Daddy hear him talking all mushy-pie about Mama. The popular girls in class also told me Mama was beautiful. "You don't look anything like her," they'd say.

But Mama looked a whole lot older down there in North Carolina.

"Hmph, I guess you do look tired. And you've put on some weight. Of course, it's been a while," Grandma said. "Let's get your things inside. I've got your rooms all ready."

I heard a sound coming from Mama like a tea-kettle getting set to whistle. But her mouth was clamped shut and she was smiling hard again.

We followed Grandma up the stairs to her porch, and she pulled open the great big front door. Ruthie darted inside. Two seconds later she screamed and ran back out. She hid behind Charlene's knees. "There's . . . there's a monster!"

Mama chased after Ruthie. "Sweetie, what's wrong?"

Grandma hurried over, too, but I poked my head inside. And there, right by Grandma's big, winding, stairs, was a bear. A real, full-grown, eat-you-alive bear. Sure, it was dead and stuffed, but it was growling with its arms out, and it was easy to imagine it grabbing you for a little midnight snack.

I ducked into another room to get away from it. But that room was filled with dead animals too. Turkeys hanging on the wall next to deer heads. A stuffed mountain goat rearing on its back legs next to a big stone fireplace. Then I spotted a dead fish on a plaque, all shiny and curled up, like he was trying to peel himself off the wall and get back to the water.

You really have to hate animals to kill them and stuff them and leave them right in your house. She'd probably love to have my turtle on her shelf too. I backed out of the room and bumped right into her. I jumped.

"I see you're making yourself at home," she said, crossing her arms.

I crinkled my nose. "Why do you have all these scary, dead animals?"

"My word, how rude. My husband was a trophy hunter."

Mama came up behind us holding Ruthie's hand. "See, darlin'? They're not alive. They're just like big stuffed animals. Go on. Touch one."

Ruthie reached out and tapped the back of an elk standing by the door.

Charlene tried to smile, but her lip was quivering.

I couldn't believe we were moving into an animal cemetery. On purpose.

"Children." Grandma clapped her hands. "Start unloading your things."

Since we'd sold most of our things with the house, it only took us a few trips to officially move our stuff into Grandma's. Mama settled right back into the room she used to live in. Charlene got the great big guest room, and Ruthie got a small bedroom with a canopy bed.

Then Grandma looked at me. "Follow me." I walked behind her down the hall. Grandma swung her hips when she walked and her pale blue dress made a swooshing sound.

She stopped in front of a door and gave the knob a good shake. "Stay out of here. This room is off-limits."

I shrugged. "Okay." What worse thing than dead

animals could she be hiding in there?

"Okay? Don't you mean, 'Yes, ma'am?'" Her big brown eyes blinked fast.

My shoulders slumped. "Yes, ma'am." I tried not to growl the words.

She walked down the hall a few more steps and flung open a door. "I had to give up my sewing room for you, young lady."

I peeked in and saw a bed and a dresser. Two dead ducks stood on top, their beaks touching like they were kissing. A stuffed owl with glassy eyes stared at me from the bedside table. A hawk hung from the ceiling with its wings stretched out. There was a sewing machine on a table and boxes of old fabric and patterns were lined up against the wall. It didn't seem like she was giving up her sewing room if all the stuff was still there.

"Thank you, Grandma," I said. But she didn't know I said it in the voice I used when I didn't really mean it, like when Billy did a handstand and asked if his legs were perfectly straight. They never were, of course.

Grandma was still staring at me. "And change into fresh clothes for dinner. I won't have ragamuffins at my table."

"Okay."

"Yes, ma'am."

"Yes, ma'am." I was starting to think the stories Mama had told about Grandma during the car ride might be some of her true ones. Grandma sure seemed like the type of person who'd make turtle soup. She probably even enjoyed eating it too.

Grandma went to help Mama unpack, and I got to work putting away the few things I'd brought. I'd sold most of my old toys at our garage sale. I was still real upset about selling my bike. Daddy had given me that red banana-seat bike when I was eight. It had tassels on the handles and a license plate with my name, Chip. Daddy had that plate made special for me.

"We can't keep all this stuff," Mama had told me. "We'll get you new things for our new home. We're going to have a fresh start down there. You're going to love it. You'll see."

But Mama was wrong. Bringing me here was like setting a fish loose in the sky. As I stood in my room with the pink ruffled curtains and the shiny wood floor and all the glassy-eyed birds, my heart slipped out of place. It wasn't home—not even if my books were lined up on the shelf and my clothes were hanging in the closet.

Laughter rang out across the hall as Charlene chased Ruthie around her room. "Say ding-dong if you're a southern belle, too, Ruthie-Roo."

"Ding-dong!" Ruthie cried. "Ding-dong!" The two of them were settling in already.

I sank onto the bed, pulled down by a hurt as heavy as a big rock.

I took a deep breath to keep the tears back and looked up at the ceiling. "I'll like it here, right, Daddy?" I twisted my fingers in front of me. But Daddy wasn't there to say, "Sure, kiddo. You'll be fine."

My throat felt tight and my face was hot. How could I survive here without him? It was bad enough to move somewhere totally new, but without my daddy too? A few tears slipped out onto my cheek. I wiped them off and decided to do a test. I'd make a wish and see if Daddy was watching over me. I closed my eyes tight. "Daddy, I wish that you'd show me a sign that you're listening. That I'm going to fit in down here somehow. 'Cause right now, my heart feels like a leftover puzzle piece with nowhere to go."

Now I just had to wait for my sign. But I wasn't so good at waiting—not like I was at nagging.

A timer went off downstairs, and Grandma and Mama bustled to the kitchen. "Charlene, Ruthie, Chip—time for dinner!" Mama called.

I hopped down the stairs, and ran through the living room, stopping in front of two lit-up cabinets filled with fancy dolls. I couldn't believe how many dolls Grandma had. I stopped counting after twenty and just studied them. Their bodies were made out of china, but they wore real clothes and had real-looking hair.

Some were dressed in outfits from around the world, like the Dutch girl with wooden shoes and a Japanese girl with a kimono. They were lined up on glass shelves in two cabinets pushed up against the back wall. Lights shone down on them like they were beauty queens from different countries waiting to be called for their turns. I pressed my nose against the glass for a closer look and saw little eyelashes that had been painted on each doll. The dolls were all set in special poses or standing near an interesting prop, like the artist doll who stood next to an easel. What was a grown-up doing with so many dolls?

"Girls, you'd better be dressed properly for dinner!" Grandma hollered.

Rats. I dashed back to my room and put on fresh shorts and a shirt. What did she think? We were one of her dolls? She better not plan on putting me in a dress.

GRANDMA'S TABLE WAS SET WITH FANCY PLATES AND glasses. We used plastic Tupperware cups back home, but Grandma's looked like crystal. All her serving bowls matched the dishes too. And the napkins were cloth, not paper. I sat perched on the edge of the chair, afraid to touch anything, while I waited for the serving bowls to come my way.

"Grandma Cooper, where did you get all those dolls out in the living room?" Charlene asked, taking the smallest piece of meat from the platter. "I've never seen such pretty dolls. And there's so many of them."

"Those came directly from England," Grandma said. "They're hand-painted porcelain with real human hair and handmade dresses. No two are alike."

"Wow. They must be expensive," Charlene said.

Grandma nodded. "Very."

"Did you get those when you were little?" Ruthie asked. "I sure would love pretty dolls like them." She stared into the living room like a dog pouting over a bone just out of reach.

Grandma smiled. "No. Your grandfather bought one for me every year on my birthday and then each Christmas after we were married."

"They're real nice," I offered.

Charlene took a sip of water and almost choked. "Chip, you don't like dolls. Mama got you a doll when you were a baby and you chewed all the fingers off it."

Mama shook her head, smiling. "You never asked for another one."

I tucked my bottom lip under my front teeth. "That doesn't mean anything. Those dolls, they're nice, Grandma. Real nice."

Mama, Charlene, and Ruthie all looked at me.

"What? They are," I said, suddenly real keen to study the pattern of roses and vines on Grandma's plates.

"Thank you, Brenda," Grandma said. "I like them too."

Everyone started chattering more about dolls and dresses, but I had nothing else to say, so I shoveled down the horrible okra Grandma had made for dinner as fast as I could and asked to be excused. I ran back to my room and stayed up there until the house was quiet and I got bored staring at the owl, waiting to see if I could catch it moving. I wrote Billy a letter telling him about the car ride down and the hawk I'd seen in West Virginia flying with a snake dangling from its talons. Billy would've loved that. I didn't get any kind of sign from Daddy, so I went down to the patio. Maybe there'd be a sign out there.

Mama and Charlene and Grandma were sitting in chairs, all huddled up together.

"You've only had Charlene in six pageants?" Grandma asked. "We'll have to get Ruthie started soon."

Worse than dolls. They were talking about pageants. I sat down in a chair and tried not to groan.

Mama picked up Ruthie and she looped her arms around Mama's neck and snuggled into her chest.

"Don't worry about Chip," Charlene said, crossing her long, thin legs. "I've already told her she's not pageant material. She needs to know so she won't be embarrassed. I look out for her like that, Grandma." She shrugged like she couldn't help being the best big sister in the world, which was not true no matter how big she smiled when she said it.

Grandma looked at me. I knew she was staring at the pale red birthmark splashed on my cheek. My angel's kiss. That's what Daddy always called it.

I ignored Charlene and watched a toad hop across the bricks in the patio. I would've caught him if we weren't at Grandma's and on our best behavior. I sat on my twitching fingers to be sure. He was a nice big toad.

"Miss Dogwood is *five* weeks away? Oh my, so much to do," Mama said, fanning herself. But her cheeks glowed that pretty pink color like they used to before Daddy died.

"We can do it," Grandma said. "It's just what we need. A pageant to keep us busy."

"I suppose you're right." Mama sighed and

dropped her head back. "It's good to be back south. I just never felt right up north. It's so darn cold, and everything's so fast."

"Of course you didn't like it. I told you to stay away from that *Yankee*." Grandma spit the word out.

"Mother . . ."

"What did I expect, though? You never did listen to me," Grandma said in a low voice.

Mama's mouth tightened. "Yes, well, you didn't . . ." She glanced over at us.

I looked back and forth from Mama to Grandma. There were more secret looks and words bouncing between them than a handful of Super Balls.

Grandma patted the arms on her lawn chair. "This is where you belong, Cecelia. Charlene too. The next Miss Dogwood!" She reached for her drink on the little round table next to her and held it up in a toast. She took a long sip and stared at my scabby legs.

I scratched at my bites. I had dozens of them. I couldn't help it. Mosquitoes loved me. I must have tasted like the marshmallow section of a Sky Bar to them.

Charlene wrapped her arms around her knees and giggled. "If you say so, Grandma. You're the expert. Miss North Carolina 1939! I bet you had all the cute boys chasing you."

Grandma started coughing on her drink.

Yuck, yuck, yuck. I got up and left the patio. I wasn't going to be part of this pageant. I wouldn't help with one. I wouldn't go to another one. And I wouldn't ever join one. Ever. Mama made me go to Charlene's first pageant, but I had such a hard time sitting still and keeping quiet that she told Daddy to stay home with me the next time. We just had to show up at the end in case Charlene won—which hadn't happened yet. Staying home had been fine with us both. We went fishing instead, and one time I caught a ten-inch bass. We let him go, of course, because of how we respected nature. Daddy was nice like that. He never would have dried up a fish to hang it on the wall.

I wanted to ask Grandma if there were any creeks or ponds around for fishing, but she was too busy talking about the pageant. So I ran across the lawn and poked around Grandma's yard, checking out her flowerbeds. I wondered if I could do some gardening with her, but it didn't look like she spent much time out there. Most everything was wilted or shriveling up. Her grass was turning brown too. I looked for a tree to climb, but the branches were all too high.

Climbing trees is how I got my nickname. I was trying to get a closer look at some neat white flowers on a tree in our front yard a few years ago. They only had four petals, which seemed unusual. I scampered a couple of branches up and reached out to pick a blossom. Then I fell and chipped my two front teeth.

Mama was real upset on the car ride to the dentist even though I wasn't even crying or fussing at all. "You're lucky it was just your teeth," she said. "Children across America fall out of trees every day and sometimes they break their legs and sometimes the doctors have to cut off those legs!"

"Oh, come on now, Cecelia. There, there," Daddy said, patting her hand.

Mama scowled at him and pushed his hand away.

But he was right. The dentist fixed my teeth right up.

"See? That chip's gone," Daddy said. "Those teeth are good as new, Brenda. You be more careful so you don't lose a leg next time." He winked at Mama. And that's when Daddy started calling me Chip. It didn't even matter that it was a boy's nickname; I was his girl.

Usually being a daddy's girl means he buys you treats and lets you out of chores. But not me. We spent our time in the woods, tracking rabbits and saving baby squirrels that fell out of their nests. Who's got time for hair curlers and high heels like Charlene's when you're busy keeping baby squirrels alive? I couldn't be a pageant girl *and* my daddy's girl even if I wanted to. Besides, Daddy always said I didn't need a pageant to prove I was pretty. He thought I was perfect just being me—Daddy's Girl.

But since Daddy was gone, I didn't know whose girl I was. I slumped against a tree in Grandma's yard, slapping away the mosquitoes. I guess I tasted good to the ones down south too.

Laughter tinkled from the patio like Mama and my sisters had been living with Grandma forever, not just a few hours. I wanted to be part of the fun, too, so I headed back to the patio when Mama called, "Time for bed, Chip. We've had a long day."

Bedtime already? I trudged up to Grandma's house without that comfy feeling I usually got on the way to my own room.

"Hurry up, Brenda," Grandma snapped. "We've got a big day tomorrow."

The sun had just set, but the sky wasn't pitch-black yet. Fireflies flashed in the grass like twinkling lights on a Christmas tree. Then I remembered the date on my calendar for the next day: 7/7/77. I sprinted across the lawn, thinking about all those lucky sevens. That date only comes around once every one hundred years. Something wonderful was sure to happen after so many bad things. Billy and I had been counting down to this day. I wondered what he'd be doing on 7/7/77. Maybe Daddy's sign would come tomorrow. Or Grandma might smile at me more than she frowned.

"Coming!" I skipped the rest of the way up to the house, tugging along a little nugget of hope that things would get better tomorrow. Daddy always said everything looked brighter in the morning. I sure hoped he was right.

chapter three

When Mama tucked me in, I decided to get brave again. I ran my fingers along the silky strip of material at the top of my blanket. "You didn't tell me why Grandma's so mean. She doesn't like me very much. And she seems mad at you." I looked up at her.

Mama stood up from my bed. "Chip, she likes you just fine. Now go to sleep." She squeezed the bridge of her nose. She did that a lot around me.

I crossed my arms on top of the blanket. "Mama . . ." I was nagging again, but I couldn't help it. I had to know.

Mama paused at the door. "It's not you, Chip.

Do you know how many housekeepers she's fired? Twenty-two. And that was just in 1955. When we'd go out to dinner, she'd make nine out of ten of the waitresses cry. A few of them quit, even. They never waitressed again and had to go to beauty school."

"Mama, I'm serious. Why's she like that? Is she just a tough nut to crack?" That was one of Daddy's sayings. He could make anyone smile—grumpy bank tellers, gum-snapping grocery store clerks, and tired waitresses. Mama would tease him and call him a charmer. But the few times he didn't get a grin, he'd wink at me and whisper, "No worries. They're just a tough nut to crack." Maybe that was Grandma—one tough nut.

I thought Mama might laugh, but she looked up at the ceiling and closed her eyes. "Someday I'll try to explain about Grandma. Some day you might understand how a person can harden up like that. But please, just try to get along with her, Chip."

"But, Mama, she hates animals, she loves dolls, and she hasn't said one nice thing to me yet. How are we supposed to get along?"

Mama's shoulders slumped. "Just try your best. Can you do that for me? Promise?"

I nodded and let out a long sigh. Mama knew I hated breaking promises. "Yes, Mama. I promise."

Mama gave me half a smile. "Thanks." She clicked off the light and left the room. I fell right asleep and dreamed that Grandma turned into a big wooden statue, standing right in the same room with all those dead animals while holding a handful of nuts.

EVEN THOUGH I WAS STILL GRUMPY ABOUT LIVING AT Grandma's in a room full of old fabric and stuffed birds, I jumped out of bed in the morning, remembering it was going to be a special day. Maybe we'd just gotten off to a bad start and things would be easier with Grandma after we'd all had a good night's sleep. It was time to try again, especially since I'd promised Mama.

I pulled my turtle's bowl out of the closet and poked a piece of okra at him that I'd smuggled up from dinner. He blinked and tucked his head in his shell. I set him back in the closet, hidden away behind a box, and walked into the hall. I stopped in front of the off-limits room. A whoosh of excitement shot through me. I'd never had such a big secret staring me in the face. A locked room I was forbidden to enter. What in the world could an old lady have that no one was allowed to see? I was just hiding a little old turtle in my closet, but she had a secret that took up a whole room.

I reached out to try turning the brass doorknob, and then yanked my hand back. Getting caught snooping around definitely wouldn't help Grandma like me more. I shrugged. *Never mind*, I thought. Maybe another day, because today was the luckiest day of the century, and something much better than a dusty old room was going to turn up, I just knew it. I backed away and skipped down the stairs, imagining what wonderful, lucky, supergood thing was going to happen on 7/7/77.

"Mornin', Chip," Mama said.

"Eat up. We've got big plans today," Grandma said.

I smiled at that, and bounced over to the table and sat down. Grandma had small, wooden chairs that forced you to sit up straight, but I didn't mind. I wasn't even upset that a box of Grape-Nuts cereal was sitting where my Froot Loops should be. "So what are we doing today?"

"We're going to town to choose material for Charlene's gown. Why don't you come along and check out Mount Airy?" Mama said.

Charlene looked at me and smiled. "It'll be fun. You can help me pick the color. It has to be just right. I'm thinking turquoise or purple, maybe."

My mouth dropped open. "That's our big day?"

I looked around at their blank faces. "It's July seventh. Seven, seven, seventy-seven! Don't you get it? This will be the luckiest day ever. Something magical should happen today. Not a trip to pick out stupid pageant material." Something sad was crawling up my throat and I swallowed hard to push it back down.

Charlene's cheeks glowed red. "Brenda! You are so selfish. This could be a magical day—for me!" She pressed her hand against her chest in case I didn't know who she had meant by the word *me*. "If we pick out the right material, I just might win that title." She clanged her spoon on the bottom of her cereal bowl and shot a mean look my way.

Grandma's lips were puckered; could've been because she was eating a grapefruit, could've been because of my cutoff shorts. She was staring at them. But it was probably because of what I'd said.

"People who rely on magic are usually disappointed," she said. "There's no such thing. And luck? The only thing lucky about today is a sunny forecast. Come into town with us. You need some proper clothes for the dinner table. You'd look quite nice in a dress, Brenda, and I'll be happy to buy you one."

"So will you come?" Mama asked. Her eyes looked so hopeful, I felt sad.

But I wasn't going shopping on the luckiest day of

the century. I'd rather go back to the dentist and get my teeth fixed again. I'd rather put in two more weeks at school. I'd rather sit next to Joey Booger Beyers at lunch, with his finger right up his nose. "No, thanks. I'd like to explore the woods around here if that's all right with you."

Grandma opened her mouth, but Mama touched her hand. "Sounds real nice," Mama said. "I know how you love nature." Mama stared at me and pushed her eyebrows together like she might cry. "I'm sure once you do some exploring, you'll see this is a fine place to live." She quickly looked out the window.

Grandma snapped her mouth shut and made that deep humming noise again.

I shoveled down my Grape-Nuts and burst out the back door before anyone could stop me. I ran down the driveway like something was chasing me. Maybe I'd find something lucky outside. Maybe Daddy would come through with my sign. I swung my arms and strode out onto the long empty road without looking back.

Grandma's road was a lot different from ours. There wasn't a ditch filled with wild flowers like we had back in New York. The woods bumped right up to the street, all thick and dark. The morning air wasn't fresh and cool, either. It was already breathing down my neck. And it smelled different, like laundry on someone else's line. The stones on the side of the road were odd colors too. Reddish-brown and round. The ones back home were gray and jagged. My feet felt different stepping on these strange rocks.

I stopped and closed my eyes. Back home I knew what time of the month it was by what was happening outside. The jellied mass of baby catfish eggs hatched in the pond when school ended. Tiger lilies bloomed up and down our road right on my birthday, July 4. Mom would pick a bunch before we went to see the fireworks.

This year we skipped the Fourth. We were so busy getting ready to leave for Grandma's. So me *and* Daddy missed the fireworks for the very first time— on my eleventh birthday—all because he was riding his motorcycle on the road when another man was driving with an empty six-pack of beer in his passenger seat.

I scuffed along Grandma's street as a car slowed down behind me. Charlene leaned out the window in her polka-dot halter top. "You sure you don't want to come? We're stopping for sundaes afterward at Snappy Lunch." Her new southern accent was even thicker.

Ruthie popped up underneath Charlene and

pressed her hands against the window. I could see Mama leaning past Grandma, smiling. They looked like one big happy bunch going into town for a fun time. I thought about jumping in the car to be part of it, but then I remembered where they were going. They'd probably spend hours in the store, feeling every piece of material, and I'd end up outside, leaning against the building counting ants on the sidewalk all by myself.

I stepped back and shoved my hands in my pockets. "No, thanks."

"Suit yourself," Grandma said.

"Suit yourself," Ruthie said from the backseat.

Mama looked away and settled back.

Charlene made a face at me and rolled up the window.

Grandma's big Lincoln Continental roared down the road, sending up a cloud of dust that swirled around me while I stood there. I coughed as the dirt blew past me. After watching the car disappear, I walked on, kicking pebbles until they bounced, bounced, bounced out of sight. There were no creeks to explore, no ponds hiding murky secrets. I didn't know what I was supposed to like about this place. I stopped and frowned. Daddy sure was taking his time showing me a sign. Then again, maybe a sign from heaven would be hard to send. And maybe it would be hard to see. How was I supposed to know it was a sign, anyway?

I thought about it for a moment and decided that when Daddy sent his sign, I'd feel it, 'cause my heart would slide right back into place. I peered up at the sky, hoping the clouds might form a shape to tell me something like a smoke signal would. But it was just pure blue up there with a lonely splotch of sun. Too bad Daddy couldn't stuff a note in a bottle and send it on down.

I walked on some more, shuffling down a little dip in the road, when a noise caught my attention, like someone tapping on a door. My throat tightened. *Tap-tappity-tap.* It was coming from the side of the road. *Tap-tappity-tap.* Same rhythm. *Tap-tappity-tap.* I kept walking and the noise got louder. I bit my lip, wanting to charge into the brush and find out what— or who—was making that sound. Not so easy to do without Billy or Daddy by my side. I fluttered my fingers, waiting for courage to fill me up.

But when I heard it again, I was more curious than scared, so I walked down the slope off the side of the road and made my way through the bushes and little trees, just itching to find out what it was.

Tap-tappity-tap.

Tap-tappity-tap.

I followed the sound until I found it. A branch from a little tree was bobbing, hitting a wooden sign. The weather wasn't breezy or anything, but still the branch was keeping the beat, hitting the sign. Words were painted on it: "Miss Vernie's School of Charm." Shivers tickled my skin and I rubbed my arms, but the goose bumps didn't go away. Charlene had talked about wanting to go to a charm school to help with her pageants. But weren't charms about magic too? Which kind of school was this?

I ran my fingers along the smooth wood. It was a big sign, and I don't know how I'd missed it in the first place. The words were faded, and it was crawling with honeysuckle and sweet peas. The two *o*'s in the word *school* stared at me like that stuffed owl in my room, just waiting to see what I'd do.

I crossed my arms and tapped my foot. Well, I'd found a sign. Was this Daddy being funny up in heaven? This was not the kind of sign I was looking for and he knew it. No, this wasn't my message from Daddy, but still, it was interesting. Maybe even more interesting than Grandma's off-limits room. My insides felt like a hopping, fluttering baby bird trying to leap out of its nest.

I peered past the sign and spotted a long shady driveway. Chimes tinkled far away. Goose bumps stung my arms again, but I started walking up the driveway. My stomach tightened with each step. I walked a lot slower than I would've if Billy had been by my side. He would've made it feel like a great adventure.

At the end of the driveway everything turned bright with color, like when Dorothy enters Oz. I saw a big house, as blue as a robin's egg, but it was dark and quiet inside. I didn't see a charm school sign, so I walked around back.

A woman stood with a silver watering can, sprinkling a great big plant. I didn't know what kind of plant it was because I didn't know the plants down south or when the flowers bloomed or the birds hatched or anything. But this plant was pretty with big cream-colored flowers. The biggest I'd ever seen.

She looked up at me, and her smile opened like a morning glory. "Hello there," she said, just like she'd been expecting me. She kept on watering, the drops spilling out like bits of crystal.

I looked around for another building, but all I saw was the house. "Excuse me, is this the charm school?" I was nibbling on my thumbnail again, even though I'd chewed most of it off on the car ride down.

"It most certainly is." She picked a dead leaf off the plant and stepped back to look at it. She turned to me. "Dinnerplate dahlias."

"I never heard of that." My turtle could crawl between the petals and be lost for weeks.

The yard was stuffed with flowerpots and decorations and statues. I turned in a circle to take it all in. Vines wrapped around trees and trellises, trying to touch the sky. Benches snuggled up to huge bushes. Hundreds of pink roses dangled from a wooden archway. The flowers were brighter and bigger and stranger than any I'd ever seen, like in a Dr. Seuss book. Wind chimes tinkled, but there still wasn't even a breeze. I felt out of breath, but I hadn't been running.

The lady stood there watching me. Her shoulders were straight and she held her head high, like Charlene did at her beauty pageants. A bad feeling settled over me. "Is this a charm school for magic—or for beauty?" My cheeks burned. Rats. This was embarrassing.

"Which would you like it to be?" she asked.

Magic, I thought. It was supposed to be a magical day, after all. I lifted a shoulder, and I expected her to scold me like Grandma probably would have for shrugging instead of answering. But this lady smiled at me.

She set down her watering can and looked at me as if I was a flower she was deciding whether or not to pick. "All students who graduate from this school leave more beautiful." She brushed her hands off and walked over. "And all students who graduate from this school take a bit of magic with them."

I stared at her, not really sure what she meant. She was either an old woman who looked younger or a young woman who looked older. She was tall and a little plump. Her hair was blondish-white, pulled up in a bun, almost the same color as her dinner-plate dahlias. Wisps of it were stuck to her moist, tan cheeks.

"What's your name, dear?"

"Brenda Anderson." I twisted my hands in front of me and looked up to the house. "Where is Miss Vernie? And who can join her school?"

Her lips fluttered into a smile again. "I am Miss Vernie. And you've joined just by showing up."

I took a step back. Then another. I crossed my arms. "I probably don't have enough money for your school."

"My charm school is free to those who need it."

I sucked in my bottom lip. I didn't need to be coming for free. I had thirty-five dollars hidden in my pajama drawer. Two years' worth of birthday and Christmas cash. I didn't even know for sure what kind of school this was, so how was I supposed to know if I needed it? My mouth was dry, and the words ran out of my head.

I figured Miss Vernie could tell what I was thinking. Her eyes got all crinkly around the corners. "The only people who find their way here are the ones who need it. You're free to stay if you choose. And you can stay for free." She smiled at me like she was the sun, granting me some of her rays. Then she picked up a small shovel that was resting against a tree and walked toward a garden next to her house.

Without any straight answers, Billy would have said this was stupid and run back down her driveway searching for our next adventure. But Billy wasn't there. I followed her and watched while she dug up a clump of red flowers.

"Would you believe I have to move all these?" she said, as if we hadn't even been talking about the school.

I kicked at a mushroom growing in the lawn. "Why?"

"Too shady in this spot. I'll try them somewhere else."

I cupped my elbows and squeezed hard. "Will they survive?"

"Flowers are a lot hardier than you might imagine. Most things are, really." She stared at me until I felt my skin prickle again.

I cleared my throat. "About the school. When do classes start?"

"Why, class is in session right now."

I locked my gaze with her, trying to see if she had squinty, liar eyes, or worse—wild eyes. Billy said you can never trust someone with wild eyes. "There's a class?" I asked in a shaky voice. "Where?"

She spread her arms wide. "Right here in the garden." Her eyes were soft and blue and clear.

I looked around for desks or books or something. Two squirrels sat on a tree branch, watching us. "What about the other students?"

She pointed her shovel across the yard, where two girls were kneeling in front of a small garden. "Oh, I almost forgot." She got up and brushed some dirt off her flowery dress and reached into her pocket. She pulled out a gold bracelet. A charm bracelet. It twisted and glinted like it was a shiny little snake squirming in her grasp. "You'll be needing this." She fastened it around my wrist.

My skin tingled. I wasn't used to wearing jewelry. I didn't even have my ears pierced. Every girl in the fifth grade back home had her ears pierced.

"What am I supposed to do with this?" I held the bracelet up to examine the charms dangling from the chain: a pair of ballet slippers, a mirror, a flower, and a heart. I wanted to tell her I didn't wear jewelry, and that trying this girly stuff on me was a big waste.

"It's the only rule at our school: You have to wear the bracelet at all times. That's how you know when you've completed a lesson—when you lose a charm." She folded her hands and looked very pleased with herself.

"What are the lessons?" The hot sun was making me woozy. Maybe she *was* crazy.

With a smile, she tilted her head. "You won't know until you've learned it."

She stared at me and I stared back. Then I let out my breath. "When are the classes?"

She shrugged. "Come when you like. School ends when you've lost all your charms."

I shivered, feeling the cold metal against my skin.

"Go on," she said, shooing me with her hands. "Join the other girls."

I angled my body toward them, but I couldn't move. I looked over my shoulder at her. "Are you sure?"

"If you are," she said, with a note in her voice like one of her wind chimes.

Not one bit of this made any sense. But I lifted my foot like it had been stuck in mud for a year and walked over to the two girls.

chapter four

I SHUFFLED ALONG THE PATH, FINGERING MY CHARMS.
I tried not to think of Billy rolling on the ground like
a beetle on its back, laughing at me wearing a fancy
gold bracelet out in the woods. If he were here, we'd
be lifting rocks looking for newts and bugs. My fingers twitched to get in the dirt. To pick a few plants
and examine the leaves. To look for moss and forgotten nests. Back home Billy and I had planted corn
from seeds in the spring, and the stalks were two feet
high by the time I left. We were having a contest to see
whose would be the tallest. He and I would be busy in
this woodsy garden for weeks. Daddy would've loved

it too. I swallowed a big lump in my throat. When I reached the two girls planting seedlings in a patch of red dirt, I faked a cough.

They stopped talking and stared at me. I waved. My bracelet jangled and I grabbed it with my other hand to quiet it.

A chubby, brown-haired girl about my age squinted at me and rubbed the back of her hand under her nose. It looked like a slug had slunk across her skin, leaving a trail of slime. "What's on your face?" she asked.

I touched the red birthmark on my cheek but said nothing. The two girls checked me out as I stood there.

"What's your name?" asked a black girl. She looked older than me, and her skin was the color of Mama's coffee after she adds her double creams. Her long legs were tucked beneath her like a grasshopper ready to pounce. Big yellow eyes stared at me from under a high Afro. Her hair could have been a dandelion with reddish-brown fuzzy seeds set to fly. I'd never seen anyone like her, and whatever words I was going to say tumbled back down my throat.

"Can't you talk?" she asked, looking me up and down.

I swallowed hard. "It's Chip. My name's Chip."

"Like a boy?" the chubby girl asked with a snort. The snot glistened on her hand.

"It's my daddy's nickname for me."

"Your daddy sure is funny." She rubbed her nose again, leaving a streak of dirt on her face.

Words clunked along my tongue, and I tried not to spit them out. "My daddy's dead."

The black girl shrugged. "So's my mama. I think."

I wanted to ask how she died, but the girl turned back to her seedlings.

The chubby girl held out her hand. The one with the snot. "I'm Karen."

I shook the tips of her fingers and sat next to her, looking around at their work. "What have you guys been learning?"

Karen sighed. "Not much. I still have all my charms." She held up her bracelet. She had the same four charms dangling from her wrist.

I looked over at the black girl, but she didn't look back. "Does she have the same charms too?"

I'd never had a black friend. We just had one black student at our school—Michael—and he moved away a few months ago. The only time I even saw any black people was when we drove into the city for the children's Christmas party at Daddy's factory. And those kids mostly kept to themselves.

Karen pointed her shovel at the black girl. "Dana's got the same charms."

Dana. I said her name silently, a tough little word tucked between my tongue and teeth. I looked at her, and my stomach felt squirmy like it did around Michael. Daddy had talked a lot about the bigots who worked at the factory and were mean to his black friends. I did not want to be a bigot. But I wasn't entirely certain how to act around a black girl who wouldn't look at me. But if her mama was dead like my daddy, I'd sure like to talk to her about it.

I kept eyeing her, hoping she'd glance my way, but I finally gazed off into the woods. "So we're all supposed to learn the same lessons here?"

Karen shrugged. "I guess. I figure the mirror has something to do with beauty. That's what I'm hoping, since I'm entering the Junior Miss Dogwood pageant."

My heart tumbled. "So this is a school to train for beauty pageants?"

"What else would it be?" Dana asked.

"I don't know." They'd probably laugh if I said magic. My hands shook as I took a few small plants from the tray. "How long have you two been here?" The sun was hot on my head.

Dana squinted. "I came last week, and Karen

showed up three days ago."

"Have you been working in the garden the whole time?" I scooped out a little hole and dropped my plant in. "Is that regular charm school training?"

"Miss Vernie says we'll learn exactly what we need if we do what she asks every day," Karen said. "She's a little strange, but she's nice."

Dana tipped up her chin. "My daddy doesn't have money for the charm school in Winston-Salem, plus it's too far away. This will do."

Karen stopped working and leaned back. "I'm just happy I'm not at home, listening to my stepfather tell me how fat I am." She closed her eyes and kicked off her flip-flops. She wiggled her painted toes that looked like squirming little pigs. "I hadn't planned to be in the Miss Dogwood Pageant until Dana told me about the Junior Miss competition. I'll show him who's an ugly lump."

"He called you that?" Dana asked.

"No, but I know that's what he thinks," Karen said. "Just because I'm not into sports like his two sons. Yuck. Sports." She flicked a piece of dirt off her arm. "It's not my fault I watch a lot of TV. I haven't found my own thing yet. That's what my mom tells him."

I wanted to tell her she wasn't an ugly lump.

Really. But Daddy always said not to lie. "Well, I'm not competing," I said.

Dana stopped digging. "Why'd you join this school then?" Her big lips turned down in a frown.

I traced my finger in the dirt. I didn't know how to answer her question. So I used a trick I learned on a detective show: ask a question when you don't want to answer one. "What about you? *You're* here for beauty pageant training?"

She narrowed her eyes until fire seeped out like a slice of light under a closed door. "Yes. I'm fifteen now, old enough to enter the Miss Dogwood Festival in August."

"But, you're . . . I mean . . . I've never seen any black girls in pageants with my sister Charlene. Hardly ever in Miss America. Why do you want to enter this one? Don't you have your own pageants?" I thought I should look out for her, like Charlene had done for me. I wasn't like other girls who joined pageants like this, and neither was Dana.

Dana set her shovel down. "It's none of your beeswax why I entered. And why wouldn't I be able to win?" She looked me over, her gaze resting on my cheek. "You think you could?"

I wanted to shrivel up like one of Grandma's flowers. "My sister's entering. But I'm not." I was getting off to a bad start with her, too, just like Grandma.

"You really think you belong here, then?" Her big eyes waited for an answer.

And I waited for an answer too. Or a sign from Daddy, 'cause it sure didn't feel like I fit in here any better than I did at Grandma's.

chapter five

Dana stood up and brushed her hands off. "I'm heading up for lunch." She walked along the path by herself before we could catch up. Karen trotted after her, and I lagged behind.

I wished I could have a few minutes alone with Dana. Daddy said sometimes the people who acted like they really didn't want a friend needed one most of all. That's how it had been with Billy. When he moved in down the street and ended up in the same class as me, he didn't like me one bit, and that was fine with me. But Daddy thought I should invite him over to do some exploring, on account of how Billy's father wasn't around. And Daddy had been right. Billy and I became friends the first time we tromped through the woods.

I walked along back to Miss Vernie's house, touching each charm on my bracelet: a mirror, a flower, ballet slippers, and a heart. I could just take the bracelet off and give it back to Miss Vernie. I probably should because I didn't have anything to learn here, did I? Miss Vernie had a big pitcher of lemonade set out on her picnic table, along with a plate of tiny sandwiches, deviled eggs, sliced oranges, and powdered cookies laid out on a white lace tablecloth. A vase filled with daisies and roses sat in the middle. I sat down because it seemed rude to leave her school right then after she'd made such a nice lunch for us. Miss Vernie took a seat with us at the table, smoothing a napkin across her lap. "So how are things today?"

Dana shrugged. "We haven't lost any charms yet, but we planted all your seedlings."

"Are we going to learn how to hold our forks and cups at the table?" I asked with a frown. I pushed an egg around my plate, waiting for the bad news. Working out in the garden at charm school was just too good to be true.

Miss Vernie smiled. "Table manners? If that's

what you'd like. Anyone know any tips?"

I looked at Dana, who was looking at Karen, who was looking at me.

"My stepfather always tells me to keep my elbows off the table. And to keep my fork out of the serving bowl," Karen offered.

"I've seen my grandmama pat her lips with a napkin real gentle and set it back on her lap," Dana said.

"Very good. All lovely ideas." Miss Vernie picked up her glass and stuck her pinkie out. "And I've seen people in the movies do this at fancy parties."

"But you don't know for sure?" I asked. "That's not one of our lessons?"

"Not unless you want it to be," Miss Vernie said.

Dana squeezed a sandwich between her long, dark, elegant fingers. "No, thanks. That sounds like a boring lesson to me."

"What do you want us to do the rest of the day?" Karen put her elbows back on the table. She stacked two sandwiches on top of each other and took a big bite.

"I think today is for the birds," Miss Vernie said, floating her hand through the air.

Dana pushed back from the table. "I'll get the buckets and scrub brush."

"No, no. You sit. I'll fetch the things." Miss Vernie popped a cookie into her mouth and disappeared behind the shed.

I turned to Dana. "What does she mean, 'today is for the birds'?"

"That means we get to scrub the birdbaths and fill the feeders. Actually, you will, since I did it last week. I'll supervise."

"So you don't have to work on posture or something like that for your pageant?" I asked.

"We're supposed to do what Miss Vernie tells us," Dana said, like I was a first-grader.

I shrugged. "I like birds."

"She's got twelve birdbaths. Have you ever seen what those nasty starlings leave behind?" Dana asked, blinking her huge amber eyes.

Miss Vernie returned with six small empty buckets and a burlap sack. "Here, girls. Now make sure you hold a bucket in each hand when you're carrying the water. Keep yourself balanced and stand up straight." She crossed her arms and smiled at us, creases forming around her bright blue eyes and her cheeks glowing pink from the heat. "That's all for today." She scurried off down one of her paths, and we went to fill the buckets up with the hose.

Even though starling poop dries up like concrete,

I didn't mind cleaning out those birdbaths. Dana rinsed off the dirt once I'd finished cleaning, and Karen refilled each bath, huffing and puffing as she picked up the buckets. I poured a few handfuls of seed into each feeder while the two of them fetched more water.

I kicked a pinecone off the path and ran my hands over the rough bark of a big tree. I closed my eyes and breathed in the fresh, warm smell of the woods and the earth. The scent of pine filled my nose. I stretched my arms to the sky and pretended for a moment that I was home.

The girls returned with the water and I went back to work. Karen and Dana stood silently, slapping away mosquitoes and examining their nails while I scraped the birdbaths.

"You coming tomorrow, Chip?" Dana said my name like it was a piece of food caught between her teeth. She pressed her big lips together.

Yes! The answer was a popcorn kernel that popped in my brain, surprising me. But this had been a lot more fun than sitting inside looking at Grandma's dolls. "I guess." I forced myself to say the words slowly and quietly.

Karen held her charm bracelet up so it caught the sun. "I ain't got nothing else to do this summer. If I stay home, my mom will probably make me read. I'll be here." Her brown hair was flat against her head, and beads of sweat trickled down her cheeks from our hard work.

When we finished, Dana and Karen wheeled their bikes down the long, long driveway then took off riding, standing up on their pedals, just like I used to on my old bike. I stepped out of the cool refuge of the woods, onto the hot pavement, and started back toward Grandma's. I couldn't hear Miss Vernie's wind chimes and their metallic whispers anymore. Seems like the minute I walked off her property, they disappeared.

And so did the good feeling that had snuck into my heart for a few hours.

Then my stomach flipped. I'd forgotten about my turtle. He'd been in the closet all day! Unless Grandma found him. If she did, he was probably gone. Or stuffed, sitting on a shelf in the dead animal room. Or boiling in a great big pot for soup. I started jogging. I had to talk to Daddy about this. How was I going to take care of a baby turtle that had come way too early?

Then I remembered. Daddy was gone. I'd have to talk to Mama about my turtle instead. Only, I'd never talked to Mama about any of my problems before. Just

Daddy. I started walking slower and slower thinking about the truth. Daddy was gone. Really, really gone. He was in heaven, and I was stuck in North Carolina. And he wasn't doing anything to show me he'd been listening.

chapter six

It felt like a cold, heavy rock was sitting in my chest as I walked up Grandma's driveway all alone. The U-Haul trailer was gone, so I guess there was no chance Mama would change her mind and take us back home. I stepped inside and let the screen door slam behind me. No one noticed. Everyone was watching Charlene look at herself in a full-length mirror pulled out into the living room, right in the middle of all those fancy, lit-up dolls, like they were watching too. Charlene frowned at the pale yellow material she held up to her chin. She grabbed a handful of it and gritted her teeth. "Mama, this color is not bright enough. It washes me out!"

Mama had a few pins tucked into the corner of her mouth. "Darlin', this is what you picked out. You loved it at the store. And you better watch it. You keep making that nasty face and it will freeze just like that for good. Happened to my friend Dolores Groves. You should have seen her senior class picture. 'Course no one asked her to prom. I don't think she ever got married, either."

Charlene stomped her foot. "It won't matter if it freezes like that. This is so ugly no one will be looking at my face! There must have been different lighting at the store. I never would have picked out something so horrid."

I dashed up the stairs and ran to my room. I threw open the closet door and let out my breath. The bowl was still there and so was Earl. I picked him up and set him in my hand. He looked at me and closed his eyes. Then I put him back, slid the bowl in the closet, and went downstairs. He needed food.

Grandma was in the kitchen and Charlene was still whining. "I can't wear this. I just can't." Her blue eyes popped open wide, ready to leap out of her head.

Mama stepped back from Charlene and tapped her finger on her chin. "If you got yourself a nice tan, this dress would just glow on you. Yes, I'm sure it would."

Charlene ran her fingers over her hair and across her collarbone. Her heaving chest started slowing down. "You think?"

"Yes, I do. You're a southern girl now. You have to have a tan. It's practically a law. Now, here's how to do it fast. Put a few drops of iodine in some baby oil. Slather that on real good, then cover one of your record albums in tinfoil and hold it in front of you. You'll bounce those sun rays right onto yourself and be tan in no time."

Mama was so smart about that kind of stuff. "Hi there, Chip," Mama said, glancing at me.

I opened my mouth, but Mama turned back to the pins she was poking through the silky gold material.

"Mama?" I sat down on the couch. The plastic cover let out a loud squeak like it couldn't believe I had the nerve to sit on it. "I have a question. A problem really." I hoped she'd know what to do about my turtle. Mama didn't have a lot of experience with animals like Daddy did.

"Ouch!" Mama shook her hand and sucked on the finger she'd stuck with a pin. "Oh, Chip. Can it wait?"

Grandma walked into the room. "Off my couch with those dirty clothes, Brenda." She swept one hand through the air like she was shooing me away. "Now, what's this problem? Perhaps I can help."

Hopping off the couch, I looked into the hall at the eat-you-alive bear at the bottom of the stairs. Grandma didn't know anything about keeping animals alive. She only knew about killing them. "Um, nothing," I said, backing away from her. "Nothing important. I'll be out back. Call me when supper's ready."

I felt smaller inside Grandma's house than I did out on the hot road walking back from Miss Vernie's. Out there I felt like a big beautiful feather that could float anywhere. Inside with Grandma, I felt like dirty old gum stuck to the road.

"Make sure you change before dinner. You'll find a few new dresses hanging in your closet." Grandma shook her head, her eyes sweeping across me from toes to nose. "Lordy, where have you been?"

The tips of my ears felt hot and I stepped back. "Exploring."

This made Mama smile. "Would you take Ruthie outside with you? She's been clinging to my legs all day."

I rolled my eyes.

Ruthie twirled in place, her ruffled dress flying. She held out her hand, and I grabbed it a little tighter than I meant to as I tugged her along to the kitchen. I rooted around the refrigerator and found spinach and a carrot for Earl.

"Oh, no. You'll spoil your supper." Grandma held out her hand. "No snacks before dinner." Her painted-on eyebrows were almost touching, like two mean caterpillars ready to fight.

Grandma was crazy if she thought I'd pick carrots and spinach for a snack. I handed back the food and stalked to my room. I sat in front of Earl's bowl.

Ruthie plopped down next to me. "Can I hold him?"

I took a few deep breaths to slow my heart. "No. Earl's very fragile. And he's a secret. Don't tell Grandma he's here." Earl was asleep on the rock in the middle of the bowl. My eyes stung just looking at him. He seemed sad. He wasn't eating and I had to keep him hidden. It was going to be a whole lot harder taking care of this little guy than I'd figured. I wasn't so sure now I could do it without Daddy's help.

"You know, Chip, you should . . . ," he'd say. But I couldn't figure out what words he would have used next. "I'll have to set this one on the burner until the solution finds me," I remembered him saying.

That made me feel better. Maybe some great turtle-raising solution would just drop into my head.

"You're s'posed to play with me outside. Mama said." Ruthie stuck out her lower lip.

I groaned. "Bring a book to look at."

She grabbed a book of fairy tales, and we went to Grandma's big backyard. Ruthie settled under a tree and fluffed out her dress, folding her legs so the tips of her black shoes poked out. She started talking to herself like she was reading, but she knew most of the stories by heart because Mama had read them to her so many times.

I found a patch of grass dotted with shade from the trees. They looked like they'd been stretching up to the sky for a long time. I closed my eyes and played the Listen Game Daddy and I had loved so much. I tried to identify all the sounds I heard without looking: two birds twittering back and forth; Charlene whining inside; a car whizzing down the road.

"Did you hear that, Daddy?" I whispered. "I wonder where they're going."

Then Ruthie started sniffling and whimpering. That girl cried all the time over nothing. Usually I just tried to make her laugh and forget about whatever was making her sad. That hadn't been working so well lately.

"What's wrong, Ruthie?" I asked.

"You're talking about Daddy. Don't do that. We're

not supposed to." Ruthie rubbed her hand under her nose.

"Ruthie, you can talk to him. I do."

She put her hands over her ears and started crying harder. Maybe Charlene was right and talking about Daddy was a bad idea. I shut my mouth and did a few somersaults toward Ruthie, and thank goodness she started giggling. "Me too, me too!" she said, clapping.

I shook my head. "You'll get that dress dirty for sure."

But it was too late. She stood up and put her head on the ground and tumbled to the side. Her white dress was stained with a big streak of green. Good thing Mama had practice getting out my stains.

Ruthie lined herself up and tumbled to the side again. "Help me!"

"Here," I said, squaring her shoulders. "Put your head between your feet and look up behind you at the sky. Shake your bottom to get it lined up just right, and then fall forward."

Ruthie stuck her ruffled behind in the air, waggled it a few times, and toppled over in a perfect somersault. She stood up and clapped, and tried it again and again.

"Supper, girls!" Grandma hollered out the window.

Her voice stopped me with a start. Ruthie was filthy. She must have known we were in for it too, because she brushed at the stains on her dress. We washed up in the bathroom and walked slowly into the dining room.

Grandma's lips tightened and turned white. "Brenda! I told you not to get any dirtier. And I told you to get changed into a new dress. And, lordy, look at Ruthie." She shook her head and clucked her tongue.

I looked at Mama, waiting for her to step between us and tell me that she once had a white dress that was covered from top to bottom in grass and that she scrubbed for two days to get it out. But she got it out.

Instead Mama frowned and yanked the dress over Ruthie's head. She started inspecting the stains and closed her eyes, shaking her head. "I'm used to you being a tomboy, Brenda, but don't pull Ruthie into your shenanigans. Go put on some new clothes, Ruthie. And you heard your grandmother, Brenda. Get changed."

Ruthie scampered up the stairs. I stared at Mama in disbelief. She'd never cared what I wore before. But I followed Ruthie up and threw open my closet. I hadn't noticed the three stupid, ugly dresses hanging in there before. One of them was dotted with red cherries, like I was supposed to be some kind of sundae. The next one was purple with a tiny rainbow across the chest. The one I picked to put on was the ugliest of all, just to show Grandma how dumb this dress-up-for-dinner idea was. The dress was brown, like dirt, with yellow ducks holding umbrellas. Was this Grandma's way of telling me she didn't like me? Guess Mama hadn't made Grandma promise to get along with me.

I came back down and Grandma nodded for me to sit.

"You look very nice, Chip," Mama said. "Aren't you going to thank your grandmother?"

"Thank you, Grandma." For making me look like the biggest dummy in all the United States of America.

"Yes, that's real, real nice, Chip. Just perfect for you," Charlene said, the corner of her mouth twitching. "And what a nice bracelet. Where'd you get that? Your boyfriend back home?"

I gripped my wrist. "He's not my boyfriend. I found it," I said quickly. "Out in the woods when I was exploring."

Charlene pushed her salad around with her fork. "Exploring." She rolled her eyes. "Listen, I know you're different from us, Chip, but don't try to make

Ruthie be like you. She's one of us. She doesn't get dirty. She likes pretty things."

Her words hit me in the stomach. Charlene had never said anything like that to me before.

Mama's fingers rubbed her temples and she let out a deep breath.

Grandma started humming again. "Charlene's right. The tomboy thing isn't going to work down here, Brenda."

"Chip's not like regular girls, Grandma. She can't help it. Her best friend was a boy. She plays in the mud." Charlene pointed her fork at me and let the silence hang for a moment. "Now, Ruthie's pageant material. Chip doesn't even have a talent. I've been singing and dancing since I was Ruthie's age. And we should get her started on lessons too."

I opened my mouth to tell them about Miss Vernie's school, but clamped it shut. I wasn't going back there to join a stupid pageant; I was going because Miss Vernie's woods were nice and she was, too, and because I couldn't stand to be in this house longer than I had to, especially if I was supposed to be getting along with Grandma while she was busy buying me ugly dresses.

"You know, girls, the Miss Dogwood Festival actually has three divisions: the Miss division, the Junior

Miss division, and the Little Miss." Grandma slapped her hands on the table. "We should enter Ruthie! I don't know why I didn't think of it sooner. There's still time; the deadline to enter is in two days."

"Ruthie, you want to join a pageant like Char-Char?" Charlene leaned across the table and tickled Ruthie's cheek.

Ruthie giggled and nodded her big head of curls like it was on a spring. Even though she was five, she usually acted like she was two. Smart girl. Ruthie had no problems fitting in as long as she acted like a baby. Everyone loves babies.

"Excellent." Grandma clapped then rested a hand on Mama's shoulder. "Don't worry. I'll pay for Ruthie's dress." She squeezed her hands together. "Oh, you two are beauty queens for sure. Just like your mama and me."

I sat slumped at the table and stabbed the potato on my plate again and again and again. If Daddy were here, I wouldn't have cared at all what they were saying. But there was nothing else to listen to but their stupid blabber. Was this Daddy's way of telling me, *Forget that wish, kid, you'll never belong here*? Grandma had come right out and said it—I wouldn't fit in down here if I was a tomboy, and that's who I was.

I slipped a handful of collard greens into my pocket and quietly slid from the table. I went to my room and crouched in the closet next to Earl. "You hate it here, don't you?" I asked him, sprinkling in the green bits of leaf. He didn't open his eyes. "It's because you don't belong here, you know. It's not your fault you ended up here like this. And it's not your fault that Grandma doesn't like you."

"Maybe he hates it here because he's living in a plastic bowl," Charlene said, leaning on the doorway.

I jumped. "Get out! Give me some privacy!"

She rolled her eyes. "Get a life, loser." She laughed and left my room.

I slammed the door and crawled into bed. I watched the sun slip away, waiting for Mama to tuck me in. But she didn't come. Mama always tucked me in. Maybe she forgot. Or maybe she was angry at me for making Grandma mad at dinner. For not keeping my promise to get along.

I glared at the owl on my night table. "What are you looking at?" He just kept staring at me, probably wondering what a girl like me was doing in a house full of beauty queens.

chapter seven

"WHAT HAVE WE HERE?" MISS VERNIE PEEKED IN MY
bowl.

"That's my turtle. Is it okay I brought him? I have
to take care of him." I'd stayed awake most of the
night, worried that Grandma would set him loose—
or worse. Bringing him to Miss Vernie's seemed like
the best solution, even though it'd been hard walking up the street without all the water sloshing out of
the bowl. Miss Vernie set her hand on my shoulder.
It felt nice. Grandma hadn't so much as shaken my
hand since I'd been at her house. "Of course," Miss
Vernie said, looking down at the bowl on the deck.

"I wonder what he'll learn in charm school?" She clapped her hands together and laughed. "Leave him up here while you girls work, Brenda."

Dana and Karen flashed each other a look. "Miss Vernie, she likes to be called Chip. It's her nickname," Karen said with a serious nod.

"It's not really a proper pageant name, though, is it?" Dana asked.

"I'm not joining the pageant," I said, hooking my thumbs in the pockets of my shorts.

"It's a wonderful name," Miss Vernie said. "A girl is most beautiful when she's herself. We'll call you Chip." She looked at me for a moment and her voice got softer. "Just so you know, tomorrow is the deadline for joining the pageant. If you change your mind."

"Well, I won't. I don't do that kind of stuff." I shrugged. "So, what's up for today, Miss Vernie?"

Her eyes brightened. "We're cleaning out my pond."

"You have a pond?" Dana asked.

"Out back. Follow me, girls." She took dainty steps down the stairs and headed for one of her paths. A group of hummingbirds flitted past us.

Karen grabbed my arm. "Why don't you let your turtle go in the pond?"

I sucked in a breath. The solution had found me

after all. He could go to Miss Vernie's pond, and not the toilet or the animal stuffer's or the soup kettle. But I shook my head. "He needs special care." Turtles might live in ponds, but this was a New York turtle born much too early. I couldn't let him go here in a totally different state. He'd probably die. I left him on the deck like Miss Vernie said.

We went to her shed and got shovels, then followed Miss Vernie down one of her shady paths into a clearing. The pond waited like a pot of liquid gold, sunk into the earth. It was rimmed with cattails. Two dragonflies darted after each other, skimming the surface. The pond was smaller than the one we had back home, but just looking at it made my heart squeeze tight. Billy would have jumped right in.

"Girls, I'm hoping you can remove these cattails." Miss Vernie waved her hand toward the water. "Sometimes a thing just grows and grows until it takes over. I know it looks like a huge project, but I'm certain you can do it. Just pile 'em up off to the side." She smiled and walked away.

"You have got to be kidding me," Dana said, staring at the pond and shaking her head. The sun highlighted red glints in her puffy Afro. She stood with her arms crossed for a while and then shrugged. "Maybe they'll pop out of the water real easy." I liked how Dana was always ready to tackle Miss Vernie's jobs.

We glared at the thick growth circling the pond. "Sure are a lot of them," I said. "But how hard could it be?" I tugged on one and got my answer: hard. I reached into the muck and grabbed the roots. The cattails were linked together in a big web. "We're going to have to use the shovels to dig them out." My arms were already covered in mud up to my elbows.

"You mean we're going to have to step in that gunk?" Karen backed away from the pond. "I don't like getting dirty. My mom doesn't like me getting dirty either. I'm not getting in there."

I picked up one of the shovels. "Unless you've got some other idea, you'll have to get in." I set the blade between the reeds and jumped on the shovel. It sunk into the mud and I felt the roots beneath me split. I tried to pull them out, but they wouldn't give up until I dug underneath. Sloshing out of the water, I lugged the hunk of cattails to the shore. I fell back, panting and looking at the puffy clouds gliding by. Tiny rocks on the ground pricked my elbows. "Okay. This is hard."

"How are we ever going to do all this?" Karen whined.

A cicada buzzed in a nearby tree as we sat and

sized up all those weeds. I stared so long my eyes started crossing, and I imagined huge eyes were staring back at me. I shook myself out of my daze.

Dana pushed herself up from the ground. "It's not going to get done just sittin' here." She waded into the water and winced as she sunk into the cold muck. She tugged at the plants, probably testing them to make sure I wasn't a weakling. She trudged back out, stirring up the mud. The pond was no longer shimmering. It was cloudy and dark. Dana grabbed a shovel and copied my move, straining the muscles in her arms as she heaved the clump of cattails. Her dark, wet skin glistened in the sun.

I couldn't help noticing how drops of water nestled in her puffy dark hair like jewels.

She stopped working and narrowed her eyes at me. "You just gonna watch me do all the work?"

"No," I said quickly. I grabbed a shovel and joined her, and we each worked on our second bunch. Karen stood on shore with her arms crossed over her belly.

"Aren't you going to help?" Dana asked her.

"That's gross."

"How do you know? You're not even in here!" Dana splashed water at her. I had a feeling Dana would have fun exploring the woods with me if we ever became friends.

I pulled up a handful of the dark gray mud and mashed it between my hands. It felt like clay. "It's not so bad. It's squishy."

Dana copied me. "Cool. Feel it!" She tossed a blob of it at Karen. It splattered at her feet.

Karen wrinkled her nose. "Quit it!"

"Don't be a stick in the mud—get it?" Dana threw another handful at her and Karen jumped to the side. I scooped up some, throwing it so it wouldn't actually hit Karen. But Dana nailed her in the leg.

"Now you've gotta get in and wash off," I said.

Karen stomped into the water. She made sure to splash us as she cleaned up. We splashed back and shook off like dogs and slapped the water to make a big spray. Soon the three of us were giggling and pushing each other. We fell on our butts and settled in the muck. We stopped laughing and started relaxing under the hot sun, our clothes and hair soaked.

"This mud is actually nice and cool," Karen said. "But I don't get why Miss Vernie has us doing this." She sculpted a little bowl out of the clay and set it on the shore to dry.

I copied her and made a small turtle friend for Earl.

Dana scooped up some and streaked it across her cheeks. "Maybe this is for a beauty mask, and Miss

Vernie was hoping we'd find it."

This got Karen's interest. She brought up a handful and poked through it, probably checking for critters or stones. She shrugged and smeared it across her face, tilting her face to the sun. "I'm going to let mine dry before I rinse it off. That's what my mom does with her blue beauty mask. She waits until it's all crumbly. I don't think it works, though. She still has wrinkles."

"It doesn't get rid of wrinkles; it's supposed to make you glow," Dana said. She rubbed a handful across her forehead and down her nose.

I did it too. The cool mud spread easily across my skin.

"What do I look like?" Karen asked.

"Like the creature from the black lagoon," I said, laughing.

We bent over to peer at our reflections in the water. We were quiet, staring at our faces: all dark gray, all the same color. My eyes flicked over to Dana. She looked lighter than her normal skin color; I looked darker, and you couldn't see my birthmark. The three of us all seemed exactly alike, standing there huddled over the silvery surface of the pond. It was like I wasn't even looking at myself but at someone else instead.

Too bad I couldn't bring some mud home to smear on Grandma and Mama and my sisters. Then we could all be the same too. The thing was, all of them were already alike. I was the only one who didn't fit, like Charlene said. At Grandma's, I felt like a thistle in a vase of soft, pretty flowers.

I looked back and really examined my reflection. Something welled up in my heart. Something about standing there with Dana and Karen, all of us looking like each other, made me grin so hard it hurt. The three of us belonged together in that pond and I didn't want to get out. This was the kind of feeling I wanted to have with my family.

"Let's get back to work," Dana said, breaking our silence. We climbed out of the pond and hacked away at the cattails again, then cleaned our faces once the mud turned crispy on our cheeks.

"Lunch, girls!" Miss Vernie shouted from the top of the path.

We had cleared at least twenty feet of the cattails. But the pond was huge. "Let's walk around it and figure out how many feet we have left," Dana said.

We walked slowly, placing our toes directly in front of our heels, walking in a wobbly line until we worked our way around the rim.

Dana frowned. "About eight hundred and

twenty-four feet. We're never gonna get this finished."

"Maybe it'll get easier," I suggested.

"Even if we get fifty feet done each day, we're talking sixteen days." Dana shook her head.

"Let's just go eat," said Karen.

OUR MOUTHS WERE STUFFED WITH CHICKEN SALAD when Miss Vernie surprised us with the big news. "I see you've all learned something today. Look at your bracelets, girls."

We dropped our forks and felt for our charms. The links of my chain were packed with mud, but she was right: My mirror was missing. Karen and Dana were both missing the same charm.

"That's strange," Miss Vernie said. "Usually my students lose different charms at different times. Must've been a lot going on out there in that pond." She looked at us one at a time.

We stayed quiet and I shifted in my seat, my shorts still damp from the water.

Miss Vernie raised her eyebrows. "What do you think you learned today?" She pressed her fingers together in front of her like a little steeple.

"You're the one who sent us out there," Dana said. "Didn't you have something in mind?"

Miss Vernie folded her hands in her lap. "There's

a lesson to be learned in everything. And it was your lesson to be learned. You'd know better than me what it was."

The three of us swapped confused looks. We learned how hard it was to pull out a cattail. That wasn't it, though. I waited for Miss Vernie to fill the silence, but she just watched us, waiting.

Finally Karen spoke. "I guess I learned I'm not just a girlie girl. It was neat goofing around in the mud. I've never done that before." She still had faint streaks of gray on her neck. "It was really fun!" Big dimples grooved her chubby cheeks as she grinned.

"What have you been doing the past twelve years—sitting on the couch in a dress?" Dana asked. "Never got muddy before . . . ," she mumbled.

Karen stuck out her tongue. "What was your lesson?"

Dana poked at a mandarin orange in her ambrosia salad. "I thought those cattails would be easy to pull out of the mud. But they were hard."

"That was your big charm lesson?" Karen grabbed another roll.

"I think it's a lovely lesson. Some things are very different from the way they appear—hard when they look easy, soft when they look hard. People too," Miss Vernie said to Dana, who was nodding slowly.

My turn was up next. My heart was pounding and the thick scent of gardenias blooming next to the porch crept down my throat. What had I learned? I got muddy all the time; that was nothing new. Maybe my charm had come off by mistake. I wiped my hands on my shorts, trying to think. But I did feel like I'd learned something. A little bubble had been growing inside me since we'd been working together in the pond. I looked at the girls, who were waiting for my answer.

Then I thought about the mud. How we all looked the same for a moment. How the pond was like a mirror showing three girls, so different but so similar, who all belonged there together. I had such a nice warm feeling just remembering it.

"Chip, what about you?" Miss Vernie asked, sipping her tea.

I took a big bite of salad. Dana and Karen watched me as I looked down and traced a finger over my bracelet. When I first came to the school, I didn't think it was the right place for someone like me. But that feeling had changed. I swallowed. "I guess I learned that you can see yourself in a different way you never imagined."

Different. The word jumped right out like a snake hiding under a log you'd just rolled over. *Different.*

I mouthed the word silently. I was the different one in my family. Me—not Grandma or Mama or my sisters. They were all the same. They weren't going to change. No way would they be joining me in a muddy pond. But could I change?

Could I be a pageant girl and a tomboy at the same time? The idea buzzed around in my head like a fly that wouldn't go away. Me in a pageant. It was crazy. But being covered in makeup wouldn't be all that different from being covered in mud, would it?

The three of us fussed with our bracelets while Miss Vernie watched us. "That is a good lesson, Chip. Very well done, all of you."

I wondered how we all learned something very different from the very same charm.

"But wait," Karen said. "What does this have to do with the beauty pageant?"

A breeze kicked up, ruffling our hair and stirring the flowers in the vase that sat in the middle of the table. Petals scattered across the top.

Miss Vernie leaned forward. "I know this much: It will help you reach the goal that brought you here."

Karen smiled and looked relieved. "To do good in the junior Miss Dogwood."

Miss Vernie raised an eyebrow.

So that was it, then. This was just a charm school

for beauty. Miss Vernie hadn't corrected her to say anything about magic. I pouted a bit, but still, the little bubble growing inside me didn't pop. I liked her school, and I wanted to stay even if I wasn't training for a pageant.

"Guess you're right, Miss Vernie. We did learn how to make great mud masks, so our skin will be its very best!" Karen said, like she was in a TV commercial.

"Oh, what a good idea! Take some mud home with you. I'll get you some empty Cool Whip containers. Good thing I made that ambrosia with it today. Seems like things always show up when you need them." Miss Vernie pushed her chair back from the table and scooted into her kitchen.

Karen played with her remaining charms. "I really thought the mirror was going to be some sort of beauty lesson, like learning to look prettier or something." Her brown hair had dried in the sun. It was wavy without the feathered, hair-sprayed bangs she normally had. She did look prettier. More natural.

"I'm not sure what to make of it. But I do feel like I changed somehow," I said, looking at Dana's yellow eyes. Did she feel like that too?

But Dana looked away. I felt a prick of sadness.

WE WALKED QUICKLY DOWN THE PATH SINGLE FILE. I was ready to get back to the pond. But when we faced the ring of cattails again, I realized how much work we still had to do. There were 824 feet of them.

"What if we worked on it together?" Dana asked. "Karen, you jump on the shovel 'cause you're the heaviest."

Karen crossed her arms across her bulging belly, forcing her shirt up and exposing her pale skin. "Geez, I came here to get away from my stepfather saying stuff like that."

"Sorry, but it is what it is." Dana shrugged. "Chip, you dig underneath and I'll haul them out of the water because my arms are the longest."

So we got to work. And we got twice as far as we had during our morning session. We spent a long time working silently. I was afraid to break our rhythm with talk about TV shows or record albums. We didn't even notice that the sun was sliding down the sky.

"Girls." Miss Vernie startled us. "What fine work you've done. I hate to chase you off, but I imagine your parents will be looking for you soon enough for supper."

My hands were sore, but my muscles felt loose and

my skin was cool in the water. The mud was comforting and so was the easy way we'd been working together. I didn't want to leave.

We sloshed out of the water and Miss Vernie passed out plastic containers so we could collect our mud.

"Can't wait to see how much we do tomorrow!" Karen said.

Miss Vernie mussed Karen's hair and Karen leaned in to her with a smile. "Tomorrow we need to start thinking about what you'll be wearing for the pageant. Will you be joining us, Chip?"

I turned to the pond and its shiny surface. I thought about the way I'd looked when I peered in the water with the mud on my face. Playing around in that gunk made me feel like I belonged with Dana and Karen. Could taking part in a beauty pageant make me fit in with my family? I did promise Mama I'd get along with Grandma, and this seemed like a good way to try.

I looked away from the water and, right into Miss Vernie's cool blue eyes. "Yes. Yes, I am joining."

The way her eyes softened felt like a hug. "All right, then," she said. "Tomorrow's the deadline. We'll go into town, sign you up, and look for some dresses too."

We walked down Miss Vernie's driveway toward our homes. The comfortable silence we'd fallen into back in the pond was gone. We went our separate ways at the end of the driveway without saying good-bye. I frowned, anxious to come back and get rid of those wicked weeds so I could see the pond clean and clear.

Then I smiled, remembering the news I had for Mama. Wouldn't she be surprised? Charlene too. I practiced all the different ways I could deliver my announcement. I was joining the pageant. I would be part of their summer project. This tomboy was going to be like them. That bubble inside me grew a lot bigger just thinking about it.

chapter eight

"Brenda, where have you been? You missed supper," Grandma scolded as I walked into the dining room. "And you're filthy again." She was standing in front of the table, serving a peach pie and wrinkling her nose. She held the knife in the air, waiting for my answer.

"I was at school," I mumbled, rocking back on my dirty Keds. My heart was practically bursting to share my news. Would Mama clap? I was sure she'd jump up and hug me.

"School? It's July," Charlene said. She poked a fork at her uneaten slice of pie.

"It's charm school," I whispered, warming up to deliver the big news.

"Charm school?" Mama asked, scrunching her eyebrows together. "Where?"

"Just down the street. Miss Vernie's School of Charm." I toyed with my bracelet.

"What are you doing in charm school?" Charlene asked while Mama gave me a funny look.

I blinked a few times. This wasn't going like I'd planned. "Learning stuff. Like, stuff for a pageant." I shrugged, and my skin felt itchy. "Maybe." I coughed.

"The pageant? We talked about this, Chip." Charlene sounded angry, and she pushed her plate away.

Mama sat up and cocked her head. "You're joining the pageant? A beauty pageant? You don't even like to go to Charlene's pageants." A little laugh slipped out and my heart fell. "Are you pulling my leg?" she asked, narrowing one eye at me.

Even Ruthie laughed. "You're so funny, Chip."

That bubble inside me popped, and my insides felt like a big empty tub. Why were they laughing? I looked down at my feet and sucked in a breath before a little sob snuck out. "I said maybe. I'm not sure."

"Miss Vernie?" Grandma set down the pie dish. "I didn't know she was still running that school."

"Really? But you're neighbors," I said.

"Keeps to herself. But I knew her long ago. She was in the Miss North Carolina pageant in 1939. The year I won." Grandma frowned, her bottom lip sticking out, and shook her head. "Anyone interested in joining a pageant should be learning from me, not Miss Vernie. *I* was Miss North Carolina. And she's gone a little daft since . . ." But her voice was overpowered by Charlene.

"Why does Brenda get to go to a charm school? She doesn't even want to be in pageants. And just look at her!" Her chest was turning splotchy.

The four of them turned to me. Man, how I wished I had some mud with me to cover us all up right then.

"How are you paying for this school, Chip?" Mama asked, rubbing her temples. "You know we don't have extra money for something like that."

"It's free. We help her with gardening work. It's nice. Real nice." My heart was pounding.

Charlene snorted. "You sure it's really not some sort of labor camp? Sounds fishy to me."

Ruthie tilted her head. "What kind of fish?"

Mama still had a funny look on her face. "I don't understand, Chip. I thought you weren't interested in this sort of thing."

I wrapped my arms across my chest like I was cold. "Well, you guys are, so I thought I'd try too.

Now that Daddy's gone, I don't . . . I don't know what to do with myself." I swallowed hard and hoped the dam of tears that was filling up inside me wouldn't bust. "I miss him so much." The words came out in a whisper that hovered over the room.

Mama squeezed her eyes shut and smoothed her hands down her thighs. Then she smiled hard. "I'm going to turn in early. Bad headache." She knocked over her water glass as she got up to leave.

Grandma watched Mama rush from the table, and then studied me like I was a spot on her white sofa, like I was a birthmark on a perfectly good white cheek. She shook her head and hurried to the kitchen.

"Why'd you go on talking about him?" Charlene scolded in a harsh whisper.

"Why can't I talk about Daddy?" I gripped the chair I was standing behind. "It doesn't make sense."

"Because it upsets Mama." She pressed her eyes shut. "We all miss him, Brenda." Her voice was thick like syrup. "But he's gone and talking about it just makes things worse."

Grandma came back in the room with a towel and started wiping up the water. "Charlene's right, you know. No use talking about your hurts. Just makes them hurt more. It's best to leave the past behind you. No good looking back at it all the time."

Charlene took a few deep breaths then opened her eyes. Her gaze was squinty and hard. "Now I have to go make sure Mama's okay." She threw her napkin on the table and stood up, her chest rising and falling with her great big breaths. "And don't bother entering that pageant, Chip. You'll lose for sure." She flipped her long red hair over her shoulders and sprinted up the stairs.

Ruthie blinked her big blue eyes at me and squished a peach under her thumb. "But the fishy camp sounds like your kind of fun, Chip."

"Ruthie, it's not a fish camp," I said.

She crossed her arms in a huff.

Grandma walked over to me and took me by the arms like she was going to march me right to my room. Instead she studied me again. "It's a shame you have your Grandma Anderson's chubby legs. Your mama and Charlene both have my nice thin figure. I'm sure Ruthie will too." She dropped her hands and stepped back, looking me up and down.

I glanced at my legs. I never noticed how different they were from Mama's and Charlene's. I'd always thought of them as good for running and climbing.

Grandma tapped her finger against her chin, nodding. "The Junior Miss division doesn't have a bathing suit competition. So no one will see your legs.

And makeup will cover that up," she said, pointing to my cheek. "Unfortunately, you don't have your sisters' natural advantages, but we can work on that." Her voice sounded encouraging. "You're not going to win, but it would be fine for us to try. Yes. It would be a good way to put things behind you and move forward."

Put things behind me? Did she mean Daddy?

"And of course, you couldn't ask for a better coach. I won Miss North Carolina and your mother was runner-up in her day. It would be a lot of work, especially with your sisters in the pageant, too, but I can make the effort if you can." She set her hand on my shoulder and smiled. At least I thought it was a smile. "It's time for a brand-new Brenda."

I felt frozen under her cold fingers. A brand-new Brenda? Why couldn't good old Chip join the pageant? My heart beat its way up my chest into my throat. She didn't think I could do it. None of them did. Even Ruthie was sitting at the table wrinkling her nose. And Grandma was crazy if she thought this would make me put Daddy behind me and forget him. I crossed my arms. "Never mind. I think Mama and Charlene are right. I'm Chip, not Brenda, and I'm not pageant material. It was a dumb idea."

Grandma pulled away from me and her lips

formed a scowl. "Very well. If that's how you feel. I suppose it's for the best. We'll be quite busy as it is." She scooted over to Ruthie and made a fuss about getting her cleaned up, even though her dress wasn't wrinkled or stained or anything.

I stood there in the dining room looking at my feet. And here I thought I'd be celebrating with everyone that I was joining their plans too. This wasn't the sign I wanted from Daddy. I wasn't fitting in. I was making it worse.

I sat down and put a scoop of mashed potatoes on my plate.

Grandma walked over and took it from me. "Oh no you don't. If you're late for dinner, you don't eat dinner."

I wasn't upset. My stomach hurt too much to eat, anyway.

GRANDMA SENT ME UP TO TAKE A BATH EVEN THOUGH I told her I was old enough for a shower. Then she made me go right to bed. But I couldn't sleep. I kept thinking about what she'd said. A brand-new Brenda? I hated that idea; I didn't want to be somebody different. I wanted to be the old me. The Chip who rode bikes with Billy. The Chip who took long hikes with Daddy. But Billy wasn't here. And Daddy wasn't coming back. Was Grandma right? Could I still be Chip down in North Carolina without Billy and Daddy? Did I need to leave everything behind? The whole thing was stirring my mind up like a stick in a mud puddle. It felt that way a lot now with Daddy gone.

I stared out my window at the moon. Could Daddy see it wherever he was? I sat up in bed and wrapped a blanket around me. I wondered what the moon looked like reflecting off Miss Vernie's pond. I wanted to get back in there and rip all those cattails out and feel the cool mud against my skin. I wasn't even sure I could keep going to her charm school if I wasn't going to be joining the pageant. I didn't want to waste Miss Vernie's time.

"What do you think?" I asked the owl. He looked like he was thinking of an answer. I picked him up. His feathers were soft and dusty. I brushed him off. He felt big but surprisingly light in my arms. "I should name you if you're going to be staring at me all the time."

I set him back down on the nightstand. "Freddy. You are Deady Freddy. Sorry about that, by the way. The whole being dead thing. I hope you didn't leave behind any baby owls."

It wasn't so bad having him in my room. He was

pretty, with big yellow eyes framed by tufts of feathers. But I still didn't like those dead animals downstairs. I wouldn't be naming them.

Quietly, I slid out of bed. I hated nighttime at Grandma's. The sounds were all wrong. The bedrooms had air conditioners, so I couldn't hear the noises outside. But there wasn't much to hear anyway. I missed the peepers back home, chirping me to sleep each night. Charlene always threw a pillow over her head when they were out, but I loved them. Grandma didn't have any peepers. Just a few crickets chirping when I opened the bathroom window to gaze out at her backyard, with its neat rows of droopy roses glowing under the moon.

But then I heard a muffled noise I hadn't heard before. It sounded like one of those dead stuffed animals had come back to life to haunt Grandma. Or a wounded bird. Maybe it was some sort of mourning dove we didn't have back home. It continued its sad song until I had to get up and investigate. I followed its cry down the hall, past the locked room, and toward the living room, thinking it might be in the rhododendron bush in front of the window.

I froze on the top stair. It wasn't a bird crying at all. It was Mama. She was sobbing into her hands like she was trying to push the tears back in. She sat on one of Grandma's stiff-backed chairs, trying so hard not to cry, all those porcelain dolls watching her like they just couldn't believe it.

I sank down onto the stair and watched her too, my fingers shaking as I clenched my hands in my lap. I'd never seen Mama cry. Not even after Daddy died. There was so much to do afterward, picking out the casket and headstone, planning the funeral lunch, and selling the house. Daddy always said Mama was so strong. She definitely wasn't a crier. Once, Mama burned her hand on the stove, and she let out a string of curse words instead of sobs. It was like Mama always skipped sad and went straight to mad.

But this time, sadness must've crept into her heart and waited until she was all alone to sink its teeth into her. And it was chomping down hard. It scared me to see her crying like that. I hung my head, knowing I was the one who'd reminded her of Daddy and had made her sad. Charlene was right. I shouldn't upset Mama. I wanted to go and hug her and tell her I was sorry—so sorry, so sorry, so sorry. But I ran back to my room and smacked right into Grandma.

"What are you doing sneaking around my house, young lady?" Grandma looked strange without her penciled-in lips and bright pink blush. Standing there in the dim light, she looked like a picture someone had started erasing. She walked to the off-limits room and checked the doorknob.

I pulled my gaze away from the door and looked at the floor. What could be so awful she had to hide it behind a locked door? "Sorry, Grandma. I was just going to the bathroom." I ran to my bedroom before she could say another word. I crawled into bed thinking about how disappointed Daddy would be with me, hurting Mama like I did. *I won't make her sad again, Daddy. I promise.*

I touched the charms on my bracelet, wishing one of them could teach me a particular lesson: how to make my mama happy. I wondered how she would look at me the next morning. Would it be one of her *disappointedinme* looks? Or worse? Maybe I'd hurt her so much, she wouldn't even look at me at all.

chapter nine

I LEFT THE HOUSE BEFORE EVERYONE GOT UP SO I wouldn't have to see Mama's puffy eyes. *I'm out exploring!* I wrote on a note. If they knew I was going back to Miss Vernie's school, they'd probably be upset. I apologized to Daddy for the fib. It wasn't a total lie. Certainly I would do some exploring. I grabbed Earl's bowl from under the bush and headed up the road.

I hurried along Miss Vernie's driveway. It seemed curvier than I remembered. Maybe it was the morning shadows tricking me. Her wind chimes were tinkling, but the air was thick and still. The woods seemed to hum. I ran toward her house, uncertain what I was feeling.

Miss Vernie was sipping tea on her back porch when I poked my head around the corner. She was already wearing a white-and-pink-checkered dress, her makeup on, and her buttery blond hair pulled up in a bun. "Chip? You're early. I don't imagine the other girls will be getting here for a while."

"I know. I was awake and thought I'd come over."

She patted the chair next to her. "Sit. Let me get you a cup of tea and some cookies. I'll be right back."

The grass was still dotted with dew, and a gang of speckled black birds settled on the ground, squawking and poking through the blades. The feathers on their bellies gleamed a dark purple color as they bounced around the lawn.

"Starlings," Miss Vernie said, bumping the door open with her hip.

"They're loud."

"And messy. Lots of folks hate starlings." She shrugged. "But they deserve their time in my garden too."

Everyone deserved time in Miss Vernie's garden. I could feel the tightness in my chest leave just looking around. Where did those bad feelings go once they wiggled away?

Miss Vernie set a china cup and plate in front of me, and sat down with a smile. We drank our tea and nibbled on cookies without saying a word. I felt closer to her right then than I did to my own mama. But how could I expect to be one of Mama's girls when I wasn't anything like her? I'd tried telling her and Grandma and my sisters that I wanted to try and be a pageant girl, and no one had hugged me or clapped or sounded happy at all. Maybe they just couldn't picture me being part of that world.

And then I realized what I had to do. The answer had found me, just like Daddy always said answers would. "Just like a lost dog, they'll show up," he'd tell me. And my answer was pawing at the door. I would work on the pageant in secret and surprise them all on the day of the competition. Of course they hadn't been excited about my news. Who'd ever seen a tomboy beauty queen? Being a pageant girl was just so different from everything I normally did, they couldn't even imagine me that way. And working here with Miss Vernie, I wouldn't be in the way at Grandma's, arguing with her and making Mama upset. Then at the pageant it would be like *poof!* Look! Chip's a beauty queen just like us. And then, I'd belong.

I smiled. Guess I did need a charm school for beauty—and not magic—after all. I looked at Miss

Vernie. "You really think someone like me can be in a pageant?"

She slid her hand over mine and gave it a good pat. "Just be yourself, and you'll be perfect."

And suddenly all those starlings flew away like they were taking my worries along with them.

I JOGGED HOME TO GET MY MONEY FOR THE PAGEANT fee. Once Dana and Karen got to Miss Vernie's, we all piled into the back of her 1965 Cadillac. It was pale blue and musty inside and took a few turns of the key to start up. "I don't take it out much more than twice a month for groceries," Miss Vernie said.

This was my first trip into downtown Mount Airy. I sat up and looked out the car window, curious about this new town. We lived out in the country back in New York and a trip into town was a big deal. Mount Airy was a lot busier than I was used to. The main street was filled with little shops and restaurants and a movie theater. It didn't seem horrible, but was it the nicest place in America like Mama had said? Not so far.

Our first stop was Town Hall. The clerk glanced up when we walked in. She was a big black woman who looked like she spent the entire day camped out on that stool.

"We are here to register for the Miss Dogwood pageant," Miss Vernie said.

"Mmhmm," the clerk said. "You girls are joining the pageant?" She looked at each one of us, and I wonder what she saw that made her frown.

"Yes, we are," Miss Vernie said, clutching her purse.

The clerk opened a drawer and pushed some forms toward us. I filled out the questions, and I wrote down Grandma's information under home address. That was my home now. But when I filled out my name, I wrote Brenda Anderson. That didn't mean I was Brand-New Brenda, but writing Chip wouldn't do. What if they called me that onstage? It just didn't sound like a pageant girl's name. *Sorry, Daddy*, I thought. *Sorry I'm not using your nickname for me.* Then, with a shaky hand, I handed over my five-dollar bill. I was officially in the Miss Dogwood Festival. A beauty pageant. My knees wobbled.

The clerk stared at my birthmark when she took my money.

Karen whistled as she filled out her paperwork. She handed it over with her money and then clapped. "It's official!" she squealed.

Dana paid with rumpled dollar bills. We looked away as she counted out the last two dollars in pennies and dimes.

The clerk frowned, waiting for her. "So you're entering *this* pageant?" she asked, counting the pennies Dana had given her. Her eyes darted back and forth between the three of us girls.

Dana stared at her for a moment. "Yes, I am, ma'am."

"What are you thinking, child? This here's a white girl's pageant." She said the word *white* like it had five letter *i*'s in it.

Dana planted a fist on her hip and gave the clerk the same squinty hard look Charlene had used on me. "There's no reason I can't join too." She held out her other hand, waiting for the form.

Dana sure was confident about entering. I tried tipping my chin up in the air like she did, wondering if it would make me feel different. Then I sighed, because it really didn't help.

The clerk closed her eyes and shook her head, handing back the papers. "Make sure you're there two hours early the day of the competition. It's four weeks from tomorrow."

Dana walked outside alone.

"Are you sure about this?" I asked, catching up and touching her arm. "Is there another pageant you could join?"

Dana pulled her arm away.

My mouth opened and closed. "I just . . . I'm just looking out for you."

Dana marched off ahead of me, her legs looking extra-long in her cutoff shorts. I watched her walk away.

"Are we going to look for the dresses now?" Karen asked when we stopped in front of the window of Belk department store. Three mannequins stared out, looking bored with the long strapless dresses they wore. "My mom gave me fifty dollars to spend."

Dana's eyes bulged. "I don't have that kind of cash."

Maybe the two of us had more in common than we'd thought, because I didn't want to waste the rest of my money on an expensive dress. I leaned toward her. "I'm not buying one in there either."

Dana looked at me and I swear she almost smiled. It was a good feeling. I followed Miss Vernie and Karen inside. Then Dana came in too.

Karen grabbed a puffy pink dress that reminded me of a cupcake. "I love this. It's so me!" It also happened to be the most expensive dress in the store: forty-eight dollars.

I didn't even look through the dresses and neither did Dana.

"That's very nice, Karen," said Miss Vernie. "Look at this, Chip." She came over to me holding a sky blue dress with tiny straps. I'd never worn a dress so fancy.

I wouldn't take it from her. "These are all kind of expensive," I said, glancing at Dana, then staring back at the beautiful blue material. "Maybe we should check the thrift store down the street?"

"This one's on sale. Just see how it looks," Miss Vernie said. She held it out in front of me until I grabbed it and went into the dressing room to put it on.

My mouth dropped open when I looked in the mirror. I didn't recognize myself. I didn't know why, but my heart was hammering and my palms felt sweaty. I turned round and round in front of the mirror, smiling. I stepped out to show the girls; I studied the ground, imagining Billy standing there with his eyes glued on me, and not laughing, either. My stomach tightened. I shook that image from my mind like I was clearing my Etch A Sketch.

"Oh, Chip. That dress is for you. I can take it in a bit. It's lovely. Just lovely," Miss Vernie said.

I kept my head down like I could hide my big smile. This dress would make me look like a real contestant—like Mama. I just knew it. But I couldn't face Dana when I handed my twenty-dollar bill to the cashier.

Miss Vernie tried holding up a few dresses, but Dana shook her head each time. Miss Vernie put her arm around Dana. "You're right. None of these are good enough for you. The girls can get away with party dresses in the junior division, but Miss Dogwood needs a gown. A gown fit for a queen. And I happen to have a few at home."

We rode back to Miss Vernie's in silence. I closed my eyes and imagined myself in the sky-blue dress with a sparkling crown on my head, Mama and Grandma waving and smiling from the crowd, and Daddy and Billy in back, nudging each other in the ribs.

chapter ten

"I JUST DON'T BELIEVE IT," MISS VERNIE SAID. "THAT gown fits like it's been waiting for you."

Dana grinned so hard I thought her cheeks must hurt. She stood on a stool in Miss Vernie's living room, wearing a violet gown that hugged her form. Of the six she'd tried on, there was no question: this was the winner. Thin strips of rhinestones held up the sparkly material. She looked like a goddess, with a sky full of stars sewn right into her dress.

Miss Vernie was a lot shorter than Dana, so I don't know how one of her old dresses fit so well. But it was truly perfect.

"It looks really, really great!" I said.

Dana didn't say anything.

"Why do you have so many gowns, Miss Vernie?" Karen asked. "Were you in pageants too?"

Miss Vernie nodded and fluffed the bottom of Dana's dress.

"How'd you do?" I asked. Grandma never said how Miss Vernie had placed when they were in the same pageant together.

"I held my own." The smile she was trying to hide broke through her tight lips.

EACH OF US WAS TUCKED AWAY IN OUR OWN DAYDREAM as we picked at our lunch in Miss Vernie's dining room. "How come we haven't lost any more charms?" I finally asked.

"It must not be your time. Sometimes a lesson is learned like that." Miss Vernie snapped her fingers. "Other times it takes a while to steep, like a nice cup of tea. And sometimes you need that hot water to bring the lesson out." She raised an eyebrow and drank from her teacup.

I looked around the room, thinking about what she meant. A picture of a handsome young man in uniform sat on her piano.

Karen noticed it too. "Is that guy your husband

or something?"

Miss Vernie closed her eyes and swallowed. "No, dear. I was never married."

"You've lived here all by yourself?" I asked. "In this great big house?"

"This is the house I grew up in. My parents' house." She pushed her chair away from the table. "Let me go get dessert." The door swung closed behind her with a loud *whoosh*.

"Would you two stop pestering her with questions?" Dana snapped as soon as Miss Vernie was out of earshot. "Some people have very good reasons for not talking about their past." She crossed her arms and stuck out her bottom lip.

"Aren't you curious?" Karen asked.

"No. Me and Daddy don't like it when people nose around wondering why it's just the two of us living in our apartment. We're just fine, the two of us, and it's no one's business what happened to my mama."

Billy never wanted to talk about his father either. Although, Billy's daddy had gone missing on purpose. I was really curious about Dana's mama. Guess Dana was like Grandma, deciding it was best to not pay mind to old hurts.

"You don't have any brothers or sisters?" Karen asked.

"I said, it's none of your business," Dana replied coolly.

Karen shrugged. "I think you're lucky. I'd give anything to get rid of my stepbrothers."

The clock ticked on the fireplace mantel as we sat there with nothing else to say. I pinched a piece of salmon into Earl's bowl, but he didn't go after it. I had no idea turtles were so sleepy. He was about as busy as the clay turtle I'd made. They sat together like tiny statues.

After a few minutes Miss Vernie came back with the Jell-O and whipped cream in pretty crystal bowls, but she never told us about the man in the picture. And none of us asked again.

WE SPENT THE AFTERNOON LAZING AROUND MISS VERnie's living room in our dresses so she could take them in and shorten them. I flinched each time Miss Vernie came at me with a pin. Dana flipped through a magazine since her dress fit her fine to begin with.

When she was done making the adjustments, Miss Vernie slumped back on her couch and fanned herself. "It's been a long day. Why don't you girls run along and start thinking about your talents for the pageant? We've got four weeks to go. You'll need to start working on them tomorrow."

"Is it okay if we pull reeds in the pond?" I asked quietly.

"You've done so much already. And it's the hottest part of the day," Miss Vernie said, still fanning herself. "I swear it must be one hundred degrees. And we haven't had rain in weeks! Hottest, driest summer I can remember."

"I don't mind. We'll cool off that way," I said.

"I'll come," Dana said, tossing her magazine aside. I wondered if Dana liked being in that pond just as much as I did.

Karen rolled her eyes. "Fine, I'll help."

"If you girls think you're up to it. Have at it." She waved us off.

We changed out of our dresses and carried the shovels back to the pond. It was still surrounded by that thick ridge of weeds.

I squinted at the area we had already cleared. "Look at that!" Glossy green lily pads floated where the cattails used to be. A big white flower bloomed on the surface of the water.

"Those weren't there yesterday," Dana said.

Karen groaned. "Do you think we need to dig those up too?"

"No! They're pretty," I said.

"I hope not. There are still loads of cattails to pull

out," Dana said. "We'll ask Miss Vernie about them later."

We stood there eyeing them up for a while. Finally I asked, "Same as yesterday?"

Dana nodded, and we started our team attack on the cattails. We got it down to a rhythm. *Thwuck!* went the weeds and the mud when Karen jumped on the shovel. *Glunk!* answered my shovel, breaking the roots underneath. And finally *splat!* as Dana tossed the mound onshore.

Thwuck, glunk, splat! Thwuck, glunk, splat! Thwuck, glunk, splat!

"We're making good progress, don't you think, Dana?" I asked.

She shrugged. I wondered if she was still mad about what I'd said yesterday about the pageant. Dana was nice enough to Karen and Miss Vernie. Why not me? I thought about how I'd tried so hard to make things work with Grandma, complimenting her dolls and staying out of the secret room. A bad thought popped into my head. If I couldn't get Dana to like me, how could I expect to get someone as tough as Grandma to like me? Could it ever feel like home if I was living with someone who couldn't stand me? With that worry nagging me, I got back to work.

After a few hours, we crawled to the shore and

examined the clouds in the sky.

"I suppose that's good for today," Dana said. "I'm going to have to go home now and do laundry for me and my dad." She blew out a breath. "Sometimes I do wish I had a brother or sister just to help with the chores. I'm exhausted."

"Too bad pulling cattails can't be our talent," I said, my breath finally slowing. "I've got nothing." I was sure that playing "Chopsticks" on the piano didn't count.

"I know all the words to every Jackson Five song," Karen offered.

"But can you sing them good?" Dana asked.

Karen opened her mouth to try, but a laugh bubbled out instead. "When my record player's going on full volume, I can."

"What do you like doing for fun?" I asked Karen. "Maybe that could be a talent."

"I've tried lots of things, but nothing's stuck. Not piano, not tap dancing, not violin. My mom says she'll sign me up for whatever lessons I want, but I don't know what I want to do." She sighed. "I like painting my nails." She spread out her chubby fingers, showing off chipped pink polish.

"I'm pretty sure that doesn't count," I said, picturing her onstage at a pageant, painting her nails, everyone sitting on the edge of their seats wondering if she was going to drop the bottle or smudge a tip. "Maybe you could do your toes too."

Karen stuck out her tongue at me. "Like I said, I haven't found my thing yet. That's why I like being here. I can do nothing and nobody nags me about it."

"What about you?" I asked Dana. "What's your talent?"

She closed her eyes. "I can sing. That's one thing I can do."

I closed my eyes too and ran my fingers over my bracelet. Three charms were still hanging from it: the heart, the flower, and the ballet slipper. What lessons did I still have to learn? Not ballet lessons, that's for sure. What the heck was I going to do for the talent portion? I had to find something, and I couldn't ask Mama for help because then she'd know what I was up to.

Once we left the pond, our easy way disappeared again. We waved good-bye to Miss Vernie and each of us headed down her driveway alone. Dana took off ahead of us without saying good-bye, and Karen coasted along on her bike. I followed slowly, day-dreaming about Mama and Grandma seeing me onstage come pageant day. Would Mama look surprised or more like happy?

My daydreams dried up when I heard explosions down the road. *Too fast and too loud to be thunder*, I thought. *Fireworks, maybe?*

I jogged down the hill. The noise was coming from Grandma's house. I stashed Earl under a pine tree and ran up the driveway and into the backyard. Birds swirled overhead, screaming.

Grandma cocked the rifle she was holding and blasted it in the air. "Get! Get out of here!" *Boom!* She fired again, pressing the long rifle against her shoulder, bracing herself on her high heels. The skirt of her dress swung from the force of the shot.

It rained feathers. Black, speckled feathers. A body dropped from the sky.

"What's she doing?" I screamed to Mama. "Why is she shooting the birds?" Was she trying to add to her dead animal collection?

Mama held her hands over her ears. "They're starlings! Awful creatures!" she shouted.

Ruthie crouched between Mama's legs, and Charlene watched from inside. She looked at me through the family room window and put her hands to her ears.

Grandma wasn't letting up. She cocked the rifle and fired again and again and again.

"Stop!" I yelled. "Stop, Grandma!"

She fired one more time and set down the gun. "Out of ammo," she said, wiping her brow.

"Why did you have to kill them?" My hands were shaking. "They're just birds!"

Grandma looked at me and shook her head. "Starlings aren't just birds, Brenda. They're beasts. They're loud. And they make a terrible mess." She waved her hand in the air. "And they chase away the pretty birds, the cardinals and the blue jays."

We stood there, staring at Grandma's lawn, now littered with seven dead birds.

Grandma picked up her rifle and walked past me. "Your mother says you have a knack for taking care of injured animals, Brenda. I'm sure you've buried a few. Take care of these, won't you?"

I looked at Mama. She lifted her chin like she was going to tell Grandma I'd never had to bury an animal that'd been killed on purpose. But Mama's shoulders slumped and she shrugged. "Use garden gloves, Chip, and a wheelbarrow. Just dump them out back in the woods, all right?"

My jaw dropped, but Mama didn't see it because she was leading Ruthie inside with one hand against the curls on her head. Ruthie glanced back at me, sucking furiously on her thumb. She'd started doing that again after Daddy died.

I asked Grandma for her garden gloves, but she wouldn't let me use them. "And touch those filthy creatures with them? I don't think so." She found me a pair of clear plastic gloves like you use for painting and a big black garbage bag. Then she went inside.

"You know, every day hundreds of children across America get horrible diseases from picking up dead birds!" I shouted, even though everyone was already inside. But that couldn't be true. I bet there wasn't one other kid in all of America who had to do such an awful job.

Flies buzzed around the mangled bodies as I stood over the birds, trying not to look at their dark, desperate eyes. I'd never seen anyone purposely kill another creature.

And I'd never missed Daddy so much. Billy, either. My hands shook and I choked back a cry just thinking about them. They would have been just as sad and mad as me, and they would have helped me clean up that nasty mess. I was going to write Billy another letter and tell him all about this. He wouldn't believe that I had a bird-killing grandma who I was supposed to get along with. This was the opposite of the Coolest Thing Ever. It was the Worst Thing Ever. And it was looking more and more like I'd never fit in this family. My heart was nowhere near being back in place. No wonder I hadn't seen any sign from Daddy. I pressed my hands against my face as the tears finally came out, wetting the plastic gloves.

When I finished bawling, I got to work. "Sorry," I said to each bird as I picked it up and stuffed it in the bag. "I'm sorry, sorry, sorry." Tears dripped off my face and onto their still bodies. I didn't understand how she could hate animals so much. How could my own grandmother be so different from me?

I carried the birds back to the woods and dug a big hole. I lowered the bag, covered it with dirt, and found enough rocks to set across the top. Then I said a little prayer, wondering if the birds would just fly right up to heaven since they already had wings.

I sat on a tree stump and looked up at the sky. Had Daddy's body grown wings like an angel right when he died so he could fly up and meet God? Maybe he was so busy settling into heaven, he hadn't had time to answer my wish. Maybe I just needed to keep being patient.

I got up and walked toward the house, leaving all those feathers spread across Grandma's lawn as a reminder of what she'd done. I could hear laughter coming from the front of the house, and I thought about going up to my room for the rest of the day. But I wanted to know what was happening to make everyone giggle. Normally I would've run to see what was going on, but I trudged along the grass with my head down until I saw Mama laughing with the girls. Grandma was there too. I stood at the end of the porch, watching. No one noticed me.

Ruthie pranced along the porch, her hands flipped out at her side and her nose tipped in the air.

I stepped onto the porch.

Mama looked over. "Look, Brenda. It's the future Little Miss Dogwood!" She laughed, like nothing strange at all had happened out back.

They all clapped for Ruthie and she took a tipsy curtsy.

"So Ruthie's definitely in the pageant?" I asked, leaning against one of the house's big columns, feeling like a cold statue.

"We signed her up today." Mama kissed Ruthie's head.

"You'll win for sure," Charlene said. "Just like your big sister." She scooped Ruthie into her arms and pressed her cheek against Ruthie's. Ruthie squealed.

"That's real nice, Ruthie. You'll do great," I said. I could've told them I was joining too. But sadness held back my words. They thought I was the girl who cleaned up dead birds, not the one who put on a fancy dress and walked like a queen.

"You'll come watch me, right, Chip?" Ruthie asked.

I looked up from my shoes. "Oh, I'll be there for sure."

"You don't have to if you don't want, Chip," Mama said. "I know how you feel about these things."

"No, I'll be there, Mama." Now, I just *had* to do good at the pageant to show them I could be part of their world, too. Because I didn't want to feel like this anymore. Like the one person they should've left behind in New York.

chapter eleven

ONLY THREE PEOPLE WERE SITTING AT THE BREAKFAST table when I got up. "Where's Mama?"

Grandma tightened her lips. "Sleeping. She's not feeling well today."

"Should I see if she needs anything?" I asked. "Like tomato soup maybe?" That's what she always gave me when I was sick.

"She's not sick, just leave her be. That's the best thing you can do for her," Grandma said, while Charlene nodded. "Now I have a project planned for us today. I need help with some cleaning."

Grandma's house was spotless. Nothing needed

to be cleaned. *Was it the locked room?* I wondered. No, that couldn't be it. I'd never even seen Grandma go into that room. Every time I walked by it, I tried to picture what could be in there. Dinosaur bones? Gold? Or maybe it wasn't treasure; maybe it was a horrible secret, like bags of stolen money or more dead animals waiting to be stuffed. Chills raced through me just thinking about it.

I fiddled with my fork so I wouldn't have to look her in the eyes.

"What I need your help with is dusting off my dolls," Grandma said. "I do it twice a year, and it's time."

I slumped in my seat.

"You're going to let us touch them?" Charlene asked, sounding way more excited than I knew she was. Charlene hated cleaning as much as I did.

Grandma nodded like she'd just announced we were all going on a trip to the Willy Wonka Chocolate Factory.

"I was thinking of exploring outside," I said. I really needed to work on my talent for the pageant, not dust dolls. "It's just that I'm so clumsy. . . ."

"Exploring. Woo-hoo, what fun." Charlene rolled her eyes and spun her finger. "Let her go, Grandma. Chip would probably just break the dolls, anyway."

Grandma thought about it long and hard. So long and hard, I started to worry she was coming up with a different, worse chore for me. "Very well," she finally said. "You may go. But you be home in time for supper. And take an apple and some crackers with you for lunch."

Charlene and Ruthie started right in, chattering about their favorite dolls and which one had the best shoes and the prettiest hair. Grandma grinned at them, while I ate my breakfast without saying a word. Like I wasn't even there.

When I was done eating, I grabbed the food like Grandma had said, and dashed out the door. I got Earl's bowl from under the tree, then ran all the way to Miss Vernie's. My heart loosened up once I stepped into her garden. I walked past the rosebush crawling over the arbor. Then I stopped and scratched my head, staring at the yellow flowers. "Weren't those blossoms pink yesterday?"

"Hmm. Might be that they were," Miss Vernie said, not at all surprised. She was waiting for us with a record player and all sorts of props set out on her picnic table. She clapped her hands to get our attention. "Time to work on our talents, girls."

"I already know what I'm going to sing," Dana said, folding her arms.

"What is it?" I asked.

She looked at me like I had asked her what color underwear she was wearing. "I'm not telling you."

I took a step back. "Sorry. I was just curious."

Miss Vernie set her hands on Karen's shoulders. "And what about you, dear?"

Karen's chin dropped to her chest. "I'm not good at anything."

I wanted to tell her she was real talented at feeling sorry for herself, but that didn't seem too nice.

While Miss Vernie consoled her, I walked over to the table to investigate the props. A baton rolled off the table toward me and fell onto my toes. "Ow!" I picked it up and ran my fingers down the cool metal, and then I tried spinning it. I liked the way it flashed in the sun when I managed to twirl it.

Miss Vernie watched and smiled. "Keep trying," she said. "That doesn't come easy. I should know. The baton was my talent."

I dropped it again.

"Is there anything else you'd like to try?" she asked me.

I tossed the baton in the air and tried to catch it. I missed. "No, I don't have any pageant talents. I'll have to try this."

"Wait a minute. That's not fair," Karen whined.

"What if I wanted to do the baton?" She held out her hand.

I pressed it against my chest and shook my head.

"I've got another one. Hang on, girls." Miss Vernie scooted inside.

Karen narrowed her eyes at me. "We can't both have the same talent."

I started twirling the baton again, and I imagined the shiny metal flashing in her eyes.

Miss Vernie came out and held up another baton like it was the Olympic torch. She handed it to Karen. "Girls, it's okay if you both have the same talent. You think there will only be one singer? One piano player?"

But Karen and I glared at each other.

Miss Vernie showed us the basic moves: twirling it between our fingers, tossing it between each hand, then up in the air. Karen didn't drop hers once; I dropped mine six times before we took a break for lunch.

Dana was eyeing my turtle when we joined her on the porch. "What's the deal with this thing anyway?" She pointed her fork at the bowl.

"He's not a thing. His name is Earl, and I found him last month."

Her mouth turned into a tight line. "Earl?"

"Yes. Earl."

"Earl." She spat on the ground. "Whatever gave you the idea to name a turtle"—she paused—"Earl?"

I poked at the lace tablecloth, not daring to look at Dana. "I don't know. I just did."

"You named him Earl? Last month? Right when James Earl Ray escaped?"

"Who?" The name sounded familiar.

She put her hands on her hips and shook her head. "You don't even know who he is? He's . . ." But she trailed off. "That might even be worse. Not knowing. But of course that wouldn't be important to someone like you." She gathered her purse and magazines. "Bye, Miss Vernie."

I looked up at Miss Vernie. Her eyes were wide and glossy.

Karen ran down the stairs after Dana. "Aren't you going to pull cattails with us?"

Dana just kept on walking.

"Why is she so upset about my turtle's name?" With a pounding heart, I ran my finger along the rim of Earl's bowl. My voice felt small. I could imagine Earl sitting in Daddy's big hands, looking up at us like, *What did I do wrong?* How could this little turtle I loved so much make someone so darn mad?

Miss Vernie shuffled through the magazines on

the coffee table in front of her wicker couch. She opened one up and handed it to me. It was *Time* magazine, with a picture of an angry white man on the cover. "He's the man who killed Dr. Martin Luther King Jr. James *Earl* Ray. And he broke out of jail last month."

With a trembling hand, I took the magazine from her. I thought my heart might crumble like an old newspaper. I knew about Dr. King. But not about the breakout.

I read through the article, about the ladder a group of seven men used to climb over the prison wall and how they were caught in just a few days, and about the bloodhounds that finally found James Earl Ray on a mountainside.

My breath was shaky. "She thinks I named my turtle after *him*? Why would I do that?"

"I don't know. But some folks didn't like Dr. King and were happy with what James Earl Ray did to him. Some say he had help breaking out of prison." She rubbed my arm. "I imagine it's something Dana and her father have talked about quite a bit the last few weeks. Just strong on her mind."

Maybe I was wrong. Maybe I couldn't be friends with Dana. Maybe we were too different and I wasn't a charmer like Daddy after all. I wanted to dive into

Miss Vernie's pond and burrow in the muck. This school was the only place I felt like I belonged, and I kept ruining things just by opening up my mouth. I picked up Earl's bowl and ran down Miss Vernie's driveway and past Grandma's house, the water splashing out of the bowl.

I ran until I couldn't breathe. I ran until I couldn't think. Then I stopped and looked down at my feet. I noticed my bracelet. My flower charm was missing. But I couldn't imagine what lesson I'd possibly learned.

chapter twelve

I DIDN'T WANT TO GO BACK TO GRANDMA'S, SO I TURNED off the road and started walking into the woods, trying to forget all my troubles. The trees creaked and groaned overhead like they were talking to each other, wondering who was there. The big rhododendron bushes and willow trees made me feel safe and hidden from the street. I stepped on bouncy cushions of moss and crept back into the forest past a bubbling creek. I poked around a bit and watched a few crayfish scuttle away. Normally I would have caught them and jabbed a stick at them so they'd grab on with their claws. Sometimes Billy would take them home and keep them in a little tank until they ended up fighting each other.

I turned over a few more rocks, and my hands finally stopped shaking. I shook away my bad feelings and tried to pretend it was a few months ago and I was back home and Billy was just around the bend, mad that I'd muddied the water downstream so he couldn't see the minnows and frogs where he was standing. I wondered if Dana would be having fun if she were here with me right now.

I picked up another rock in the creek, and jackpot! I found the Coolest Thing Ever. Ever! A long, sparkly rock with a hole right in the middle like it was meant for a key. Billy would have given me his Magic 8 Ball for that rock.

I set the rock in Earl's bowl and found a tree with a branch just low enough that I might be able to climb it. I left the bowl on the ground and jumped until my hand caught hold of the branch. I pulled myself up. I made it up two more branches until I settled on a long wide arm of the tree. I imagined it was holding me there like I was queen of the woods. Hovering above the ground like that felt right; I was up above the world, all alone. And I realized I was a little closer to Daddy up there. So I stayed in that tree, watching the sun move across the sky.

It almost felt like I belonged there, all by myself in that tree where there was no one to fight with or say the wrong thing to.

"BRENDA? IT IS EIGHT O'CLOCK. IT'LL BE DARK SOON! Where have you been, young lady?" Grandma stood in the doorway of the family room with her arms crossed. She tapped her foot in her pointy white shoe.

"I got lost in the woods." I didn't actually get lost-lost, but I did get lost in my thoughts, so I wasn't lying. I coughed. My throat was dry and I was so thirsty, I would have taken a swig from a fishbowl. "I'm just going to bed."

"That's right you are. If you don't show up for supper, you don't get supper."

"Okay."

"You say 'Yes, ma'am' in my house."

I waited for Mama to jump up and tell Grandma that sometimes I got so caught up in my adventures, I came home after dark, but she just sat on the sofa with sad eyes. I bit my lip and nodded. "Yes, ma'am." Mama was probably real disappointed in me. I wasn't doing so good at getting along with Grandma, even after I had promised I would. I waited for Grandma to go back to her TV show in the family room, then dashed out to the porch to sneak Earl back inside.

The familiar theme song from our Sunday night show floated out from the family room. I saw the blue light of the television glow against Mama's face as she huddled on the couch with Charlene and Ruthie. Grandma sat in her rocking chair, with a bowl of popcorn on her lap.

This is how we spent our weekends back home. Only, I would be on the floor in a beanbag chair watching too. Right next to Daddy.

I ran off to bed without anyone even noticing me.

THE NEXT MORNING, I WOKE UP EARLY, HUNGRY FOR breakfast. I peeked out the window. The sky was purple and the house was quiet. Then my stomach growled and I thought about Earl. He must be hungry too. I opened the closet door and pulled out his bowl.

My stomach turned inside out. Earl was gone. The keyhole rock was propped up against the side of the bowl. He must have climbed up it and right out.

I tore through the closet, pulling out bags and boxes, but I didn't see him. My door was closed, so he had to be in the room. But then I looked more closely at the crack under the door. He could have slipped right under it. He could be anywhere. "Have you seen him, Deady Freddy?" I asked the owl. He was no help as usual.

I double-checked my room, crawling around on my hands and knees. He wasn't in there. I searched the hall and the bathroom. I didn't see him on the steps going downstairs and he wasn't that fast. He had to be upstairs. And the first door I looked at, right across from mine, was the off-limits room.

I stood quietly in the hall. It was so early everyone else was still asleep. I'd have to sneak in there. If Earl was inside, I needed to get him out. Luckily, Billy had shown me how to open a locked door when we were snooping around his house looking for hidden Christmas presents. I tiptoed into the bathroom, slid open a drawer on the vanity, and searched for a big bobby pin. There were plenty to choose from in the jumble of rollers and hair clips. I straightened one out, went back in the hall, and stood in front of the door hoping my hand would stop shaking. Taking a deep breath, I stuck the bobby pin in the lock on the off-limits room doorknob, and turned it like a key. I jumped when I heard the lock pop, and I scanned the hallway. Had Grandma heard it too? She had a better chance of hearing my heart, it was pounding so hard.

My hand closed around the cold metal knob and I gripped it, frozen in place. Something felt stuck in my throat and I tried to swallow. I closed my eyes and turned the knob. Slowly, I pushed open the door and stood there for a moment with my foot in the air before setting it down inside the room. It was dark, with the shades drawn. Spider webs hung down from the ceiling like gauzy drapes. The room smelled musty and I sneezed. I froze, wondering if anyone had heard that. My heart was beating faster and faster the longer I stood there.

Once my eyes adjusted to the dim lighting, I took a better look around the room. A big desk sat at one end covered with papers and trinkets: a brass elephant, a pencil holder, and a crystal paperweight shaped like a duck. On the other side of the room a cabinet with a blanket covering it was pushed up against the wall. Were all of Grandma's secrets hiding in there? I wanted to peek behind that blanket, but there were boxes stacked up all over the floor and against the walls, so I couldn't make it across the room.

Pictures hung on the walls from the floor up to the ceiling. I crept over for a closer look. There were so many, my eyes didn't know where to settle. I paused in front of a wedding picture. Grandma's wedding picture. She wasn't smiling, but the older man next to her was. I wondered if that was her daddy or her husband. My grandpa, the dead animal trophy hunter.

The man in the photo was bald, with a big belly. Grandma looked just like Charlene, with dark hair curling past her shoulders. I ran my finger across the glass, leaving a streak in the dust. Nearby, there was another picture with a whole bunch of bunnies and chickens. I wanted to investigate, but I heard a noise behind me that sounded like one of the dead animals growling.

I jumped. It wasn't an animal; it was worse. Way worse. It was Grandma, making that deep humming noise of hers. And Earl was right by her feet. I dove and grabbed my turtle before she saw him.

"I told you this room is off-limits!" she hollered. "What do you think you're doing?"

I looked up at her from the floor, cupping Earl in my hands. "I . . . I . . . I . . ."

I heard footsteps coming down the hall. Soon Mama was in the doorway, tying her robe. "What's going on in here?"

Grandma pointed at me. "This little hooligan of yours broke in my room and started snooping around. I told her this room was off-limits!"

"Brenda, what are you doing in here?" I was ready for Mama to holler, but her voice was calm and quiet. Sad, almost.

My mouth opened and closed like a fish stuck on

a hook, but how could I explain?

"She stole something," Grandma said. "What do you have there?"

My stomach tumbled like it was rolling down a hill. I slowly opened my shaking hands. "It's just my turtle," I whispered.

Grandma's face turned red, like a sudden sunburn. "I do not want animals in my house! Get rid of it! Get rid of it now!"

But I was staring back at the pictures and, as usual, the wrong words worked their way out. "Who's that in the wedding picture with you, Grandma? Your daddy or your husband?"

Her red face turned white, but she didn't answer.

"That's Grandpa. That was my daddy." Mama closed her eyes and rubbed her temples. "He died before any of you were born."

"Why do you keep all this stuff locked in here?" I asked. "Why is it off-limits?"

Grandma took a big breath of air like she was getting ready to dunk underwater. "This is none of your business. Now don't let me catch you in here again. And get rid of that," she said, pointing at my turtle. Her voice was shaking so much, I couldn't tell if she was going to cry or scream. "See to it that that thing is gone, Cecelia. And keep her out of here." Her voice cracked. Grandma pushed us out of the room and slammed the door. She turned the knob to make sure it was locked. Then she went back to her room and slammed that door too.

Ruthie and Charlene had been peeking out of their rooms, and they quickly ducked back inside them.

Mama and I stood there in the hall staring at each other. "Why did Grandma marry someone so old?" I asked in a whisper.

Mama leaned against the door. "It's a very long story."

I closed my hand around Earl's shell. His head and feet were pulled all the way in so it felt like I was holding a rock. "Is it one of the reasons Grandma got all hardened up like you said?"

Mama sighed. "You could say so." I waited for her to tell me more, but she didn't. "I asked you to get along with your grandma. You promised. I don't need this stress, Chip."

"I know, Mama. I won't do it again." Although, I was still itching to know what was in that cabinet.

Normally, Mama would've yelled, or marched me to my room, but she just sighed again. "Now, what are you going to do with that?" She pointed to Earl.

I shrugged. I couldn't go back to Miss Vernie's and

let him go. With Dana so mad at me about my turtle's name, I didn't dare show up with him again, if I even dared to go back at all. I'd made a mess of things there. "What if I got a better cage for him, so he won't get out? Maybe keep him outside?"

Mama frowned. "I don't know. Let's check out the pet store in town. Right after breakfast."

I crossed my fingers. *Please let me keep him.* I'd made a promise to Daddy, too, to keep this turtle safe, and I wasn't going to break it.

THE SUN WAS JUST STARTING TO PEEK OUT OVER THE trees, and I took Earl outside and let him crawl in the grass. Birds hopped around, yanking on worms. "For a little guy who doesn't do too much, you sure have caused me an awful lot of trouble," I whispered to Earl. "First Dana, now Grandma. And here I am just trying to help you." He was so small, the grass must've seemed like a jungle to him as he pushed the blades down with his little legs and tiny claws.

I lay on my belly, watching Earl and wondering if Dana would come back to school. Did she just take off for the day or for good? I admired her for believing in something so strongly she'd leave Miss Vernie's. Maybe she was a nut I never could crack and maybe we'd never be friends, but I still liked that she was strong and proud. I was glad I'd met her even if she didn't feel the same way about me. I picked a small daisy that was sprouting up out of Grandma's grass and twirled it between my fingers. I thought about Karen and how hard she was working at something new, and why it was important to her to show her stepfather she was special. I felt like I was starting to understand her and Dana better. And that made my good feelings for them grow.

Grow. Like a flower? Like the charm I'd lost? I glanced at the house and saw Grandma's silhouette in the bathroom. The more I knew about Dana and Karen, the more I understood why they were the way they were. And the more I understood about them, the more I liked them. Maybe other people could grow on me too. Was that my lesson?

I sat up, excited by the idea. Possibly even Grandma could grow on me. She was mad at me and had said some nasty things, but being in her room like that made me want to know her and all her secrets better. And if people could grow on *me*, then maybe *I* could grow on other people. Like Grandma. Then maybe I really could get along with her and make Mama happy. Was that the whole key? I looked back at the house. Grandma was gone from the window. One thing was for sure: I had to get back in the off-limits room soon. There had to be something in there that would help me and Grandma grow on each other.

Hopping up from the ground, I scooped up Earl and his bowl and went inside to get ready for town and to start making things right with Grandma. I wasn't a hooligan. I had to prove to her that I was worth knowing too.

When I got to my room, I pulled out one of the dresses she'd bought for me to wear into town. I was going to miss a day at charm school, but patching things up with Grandma was more important.

Me, Ruthie, and Charlene were sitting in the backseat of Grandma's Cadillac, ready to go, when Grandma turned around and narrowed her eyes at the bowl on my lap. "We're not taking that thing in my car."

Ruthie sat between me and Charlene. She snuggled against me and looked in the bowl. She poked Earl with her finger.

"Leave him be, Ruthie!"

She crossed her arms and pouted.

"Mother, Brenda's bringing it to a pet store," Mama said. "We're going to see what we can do."

Grandma tightened her mouth and backed out of the driveway. She flashed me mean looks in her rearview mirror as she drove. She didn't even say anything about the purple dress with the rainbow I was wearing. Sure, there were a pair of shorts underneath it, but she didn't know that. I also had my keyhole rock in one of the pockets to mail to Billy, but she didn't know that, either.

"I certainly hope we get some rain soon," she said. "I'm breaking my back watering my roses and it doesn't seem to make a lick of difference. They're still droopy."

I quickly pressed my nose against the window, thinking about all the work I was doing for Miss Vernie. If Grandma knew how much I like working in gardens, she could ask me for help with that instead of dusting dolls. I rubbed the thumb along the rim of the bowl. All right. I was going to try to be nice. I took a deep breath and hoped my words came out right. It was the first time we'd talked since the fight in the off-limits room. "I know how you feel, Grandma. I planted corn back home before we moved here. I sure hope somebody's watering it. Maybe I could help you with your roses."

Grandma flipped her hand in the air. "It's not the same thing at all. Vegetables and crops can adapt to severe weather. My roses are delicate and vulnerable. It takes a skilled gardener to care for them."

"Well, you could tell me what to do," I offered.

"That won't be necessary," Grandma said.

I leaned my head against the window. Guess it would take some time for me to grow on Grandma. Maybe that would change though, once she saw me at the pageant. Being a beauty queen seemed like my only hope with her.

I CARRIED EARL INTO THE PET SHOP, AND RUTHIE RAN right past me to the kittens. Charlene and Grandma walked down to the department store to look for shoes while Mama and I talked to the old man behind the counter.

"Excuse me," Mama said with a big smile. Most people helped Mama when she gave them that smile. "We've got a turtle who needs a new home. Do you have any setups that could keep this little guy from getting away?"

The man rubbed his big spotted hand along the back of his head and frowned. "We used to have real nice plastic palm tree cages for little turtles. But we can't sell baby turtles anymore. FDA just banned them."

Was this some weird southern thing? "Why?" I asked.

"Turtles carry salmonella and kids can put the

tiny ones in their mouths and get sick."

Mama pressed her hands to her mouth. "They carry a disease?"

"That's what they say."

"So they're illegal?" she whispered.

"Only to sell them. Nothing illegal about keeping it. Might not be very smart, though."

I backed away from the counter, a sick feeling bubbling up in my stomach.

Mama folded her hands in front of her. "Ruthie could get sick."

"Let me see your turtle, darlin'," the old man said.

I shook my head and clutched the bowl against me.

He shifted on his stool. "That don't look like the best home for him."

With a great big sigh, I set the bowl on the counter. He scratched his head again. "What are you feeding him?"

"Vegetables. Lettuce and stuff."

"He needs dried flies too. And he can only swallow food when he's in the water. Did you know that?" He pressed his mouth into a tight line.

"No, sir." I didn't even bother trying to stuff my tears away. I wasn't taking care of Earl. I was killing him.

"He should be in an aquarium with a light for heat and enough water to swim."

I felt like sitting on the floor and crying, but instead I squared my shoulders and tried to sound real serious and mature. "Mama, can we get one? He won't be able to get out. I promise."

Mama shook her head. "It's not safe."

"But he's my responsibility. . . . Daddy would want me to. . . ." I shuddered, trying to pull in a deep breath. I wasn't supposed to talk about Daddy anymore.

Mama took a step toward me. "Chip . . ."

"I'll even buy it. I've got ten dollars. . . ." My lip wobbled. "Please."

Mama closed her eyes for a long time, pinching the bridge of her nose. "I can't let anything else bad happen to this family. You have to get rid of the turtle." She said it in the quietest voice I'd ever heard.

I stared at Earl, his shell divided up into patches like a quilt. I couldn't take care of him. I'd failed. I choked back my cries. A few months ago I would have whined and stomped my foot and nagged Mama until she changed her mind. Well, that's what the old Chip would've done. But I wanted to make Mama happy. And Grandma too. So I had to choose: keep my promise to Daddy or keep my promise to Mama. I'd never broken a promise to Daddy before, but I was going to have to. I wasn't just living in a different place with different people, I was a different person too. I was training for a pageant, and I couldn't take care of animals anymore. Plus, Daddy hadn't sent me any signs that old Chip was going to fit in. My heart wasn't slipping back into place at all. Grandma was right when she said I had to be Brand-New Brenda down in North Carolina. I didn't have a choice. "I'll find a place to let him go." My voice was so small I wasn't even sure if the words made it out of my mouth.

Mama rubbed my shoulder. "Thanks, honey."

The cool rock I'd found in the creek was in the pocket of my shorts, poking my hip under my dress. I cleared my throat. "Mama, I've got something to mail. Can we go to the post office?" I tried to make my voice sound normal, but my throat was thick.

Mama just nodded and we left the pet store. We walked a little ways down the street to the post office. We didn't talk at all. Mama stared straight ahead of her, holding Ruthie's hand.

The postal clerk gave me a small box and I set the rock inside. I pulled a flyer off the bulletin board for a chicken barbecue two weeks past. Then I grabbed a pen from the counter and started writing.

Dear Billy,

I found the new Coolest Thing Ever and wanted you to have it since you gave me the round rock. I'm not having any fun down here. How about you?

Your pal,

Chip

Then I crossed out "Chip" and wrote "Brenda."

PS I'm going by Brenda now. I'm a brand-new Brenda.

I stared at those words until they were blurry. Then I folded up the paper, stuffed it into the box, and handed my package to the clerk. Mama squeezed my shoulder. "All set, Chip?"

"Mama, call me Brenda from now on."

"Whatever for?"

"Chip's who I was back in New York. I'm a brand-new Brenda down here." Chip was gone, just like Daddy was.

She nodded slowly and let out a long, tired breath. "If that's what you want. Sometimes, new starts are a good thing."

"I'm trying, Mama. I'm trying."

When we got home, I grabbed a book and ran down the road, back into the woods, and climbed that tree of mine by the creek. I didn't even do any exploring back there. Didn't seem like something Brand-New Brenda should do.

chapter thirteen

I ROLLED AROUND IN BED ALL NIGHT LONG, TANGLING the sheets around my legs, wondering if I should go back to Miss Vernie's after everything that happened with Earl and Dana. But when I saw my family talking and laughing at breakfast, I sat down and tried to join in. They were joking about a blanket Mama once tried to knit.

Then Charlene talked about a project she'd made in home ec, and Ruthie said she wanted to learn to knit. I didn't know what to say. I felt like an orange in an apple crate.

"Is knitting hard?" I asked. "Maybe you could

teach me someday, Mama." I figured that might be a way for us to spend time together since she liked it so much.

Mama frowned. "It can be. You don't have the patience for knitting, Chip." She chuckled. "I'm sure you couldn't sit still long enough."

Mama was used to dealing with just Ruthie and Charlene. She didn't have time to squeeze me in, too, and I sure didn't want to add more stress to her life.

"You're probably right," I said. I grabbed a muffin and headed for the door. "I'm going exploring."

No one even protested. "You be careful out there. Thousands of kids get hurt in the woods every day and are never heard from again," Mama hollered after me.

"I will." I walked up the street and down Miss Vernie's driveway, the trees whispering above me. I clutched the bowl, hoping I wasn't making a mistake bringing Earl back there, but I had to get rid of him. My knees were just barely holding me up as I walked into the garden. Karen tossed her baton in the air while Dana sat on the porch. I was so glad to see she'd come back. I took a deep breath and walked right up to them. A ray of light broke through the clouds so I was standing in a patch of sunshine.

"Chip!" Karen dropped her baton and ran over.

"Where were you yesterday?"

"I wasn't feeling well. And I'm not going by Chip anymore."

Miss Vernie folded down her paper to look at me. "I rather liked your nickname. Why the sudden change?"

I felt my lips tightening. "Brenda is more appropriate for a pageant, don't you think?"

"I think you should do what feels most comfortable for you," Miss Vernie said.

I tipped up my chin. "Well, Brenda feels comfortable." That's what people called me before I chipped my teeth, anyway. I must've been comfortable with it back then.

Karen blinked at me. "Um, okay, Brenda." She walked up the porch with me. "How's your turtle?"

Dana froze, keeping her eyes on the same spot of her page.

"Mama wants me to get rid of him. I said I'd let him go in your pond, Miss Vernie." My voice cracked.

Miss Vernie put down her paper and looked at me. "That turtle's something special to you, isn't he?"

I nodded, tears dripping down my face.

"Why don't you leave him here with me? I'll take care of him for you until you figure out something that doesn't hurt your heart so much."

I ran to her and wrapped my arms around her. She patted my back. She smelled like sugar and lavender and something that softened my heart. Picking up the bowl, she set Earl on the corner of her covered deck.

Miss Vernie cupped my cheek in her hand. Then she sat down and picked up her paper again. "Did you girls know they're going to test the space shuttle this month with the first manned flights? Isn't that exciting?"

Miss Vernie was always telling us about news stories. I couldn't believe how many newspapers she read. There were old copies from cities all around the country. But I knew she was just changing the subject right then on my account.

"Wow," Karen said, trying to sound interested while she searched for her baton in the grass.

Dana hadn't looked up yet, but Miss Vernie put her hand on her shoulder. "Shall we work on the choreography for your song?"

Dana shook her head. "I'm just going to sing. No moves. My song will be enough." She stood up. "I'm heading down to the pond."

"We'll come with you," I suggested, hoping Dana wouldn't mind.

Karen found her baton and set it on the deck. "Sounds good to me."

Dana didn't answer, but she grabbed a shovel and followed us. We were tromping down the path through the woods when something caught my eye. It was a golden glow far off between the trees. I stopped and squinted. "What's back there?"

Karen put her hands on her hips. "I'm not sure. Looks like there might be a path headed that way."

I wrapped my hand around a tree branch and gazed down the path. "There's one way to find out."

Dana shook her head. "Let's just get to work."

But Karen and I ran off along the trail toward the light. I could hear Dana following behind us, twigs snapping under her feet. We pushed back branches and vines until the forest ended in a big open field covered in white. "Is that snow?" I whispered.

Karen stood there with her mouth open. Dana finally caught up to us and studied the field. "Wishing flowers!" she said.

Then it clicked. "Dandelions! Thousands of them!" I took a few steps forward so I could pick one. I twirled it between my fingertips and watched the fuzzy seeds fly. They floated up, up, and away.

Karen giggled and ran through the field, sending clouds of white into the air.

"Karen, you're wasting wishes!" Dana yelled after her.

"How do you know I'm not making wishes while I'm running?" Karen spun around, kicking at the flowers to make the seeds sail.

I stepped into the field, the puffy flower heads tickling my legs. Then I stooped over and ran my fingers along the tops of the dandelions, releasing their tiny parachutes. Whenever I found a dandelion back home, I'd try to flick off the head and see how far it would go. But this seemed like a place to whisper wishes. So I grabbed a handful of flowers and held them up to the sky, shaking them back and forth hoping Daddy could see. Maybe that would remind him of my wish, because I still didn't fit in right anywhere, and I still hadn't seen a sign. Maybe I needed a new wish. "Help me make things right with Dana. Help me be like Mama and Charlene and Ruthie. Help me be one of Mama's girls." And I blew on those flowers like they were birthday candles, hoping my words would make it to heaven.

Dropping the bare stems, I looked over at Dana, who was studying a flower, blowing on it softly, and releasing the seeds a few at a time. Karen was still shrieking and running through the field like a crazy person. For someone who normally likes just sitting around, she was having a good time.

I looked up at the thousands of dandelion seeds

floating above us like snowflakes going the wrong way—up toward the sky instead of down to the ground. I walked over to Dana. "What are you wishing for?"

She didn't look at me. "What makes you think I'm wishing for anything?"

"Everyone has a wish, don't they?"

Dana lifted a shoulder.

I took a deep breath. "I'm sorry about the thing with my turtle." I tied a flower stem into a knot. "I forgot who James Earl Ray was. I didn't know he broke out of jail. We haven't really been keeping track of that kind of stuff at my house."

Dana snorted, tossing a blown-out dandelion to the ground. "Right. That's not something white folks would need to keep track of."

"No." I nibbled on my lip. "It's just that lately we've had our own problems." I closed my eyes and waited for her to say something.

Finally she said, "Let's just forget about it." She picked another flower and started blowing.

"Thanks." The corners of my mouth were twitching into a smile. Was one of my wishes already coming true? "So what's your wish?"

She put a hand on her hip. "Shush! You don't talk about them if you want them to come true."

"Are you wishing your mama was still with you?" I sure hoped she wouldn't get mad at my question.

She gave me a look. "Maybe. But I just don't like talking about it." She blew away the last seed on her flower.

"Well, like I told you guys, my daddy died, and I know how hard it can be losing someone you love. And feeling all alone—like your heart has a deep end you didn't even know about."

She looked at me and her eyes softened. "I know that feeling." I hoped she might say something more, but Karen galloped toward us, a white cloud in her wake. "This is so cool!"

Dana scolded her. "Girl, you tore up that whole field."

"It was fun! And I had a lot of wishing to do," Karen said. "I wished for a pool in our backyard and a crown at the pageant and to grow four inches by next year."

"Now that you told us, you're never going to get those things," Dana said.

"That's just a lie. I think the more people you tell, the more likely it is to come true," Karen said, nodding. "But I forgot to wish for a boyfriend in sixth grade!" She covered her mouth and giggled. "Come on!" She grabbed me and Dana by the hands and pulled us back into the field. We had to run to keep up with her, and soon enough we were tearing trails through the dandelions too, the heads tickling our calves, the air around us looking like a snowstorm. We ran until we tumbled to the ground, panting.

Karen held up her arms. "We're totally covered in fuzz!"

We looked at each other, giggling. There wasn't a patch of our skin that didn't have dandelion seeds stuck to it. It reminded me of the mud back in the pond, only this time we were all fuzzy and white instead of slick and dark.

"What a mess," Dana said, picking fuzzes off her arm. "We should get back so we can work on the pond."

We tried brushing away the seeds, but there were too many. The three of us walked back to the path, looking like we'd rolled in lint.

"Did you make a wish?" Karen asked me.

I wasn't ready to be sharing my wishes. "I did, but I'm not telling. I hope yours comes true."

She giggled. "Me too. Man, this is better than watching TV. I'm so glad I found Miss Vernie's school."

I stopped walking. "What do you mean you found it? Like in a newspaper ad?"

She shook her head. "No. I wasn't even looking for a charm school. My mom and I were going to the dentist and we were arguing about whether I need braces or not. I don't. I totally don't need braces and the dentist agrees, but my mom wants my teeth to be perfect. Well, Mom didn't even realize she'd turned down the wrong road, which is weird because she never gets lost."

We started down the path again, listening to Karen's story, not even paying attention where we were going. "So then what happened?" I asked.

Karen snapped a branch off a dead tree and started using it as a walking stick. "When she finally figured out we were going the wrong way, she turned the car around and I saw the sign. It was like a ray of sun was lighting it up or something. So I begged my mom to check it out. She drove her car up the driveway and we met Miss Vernie."

My heart was beating double-time. "And you joined that day?"

"When my mom found out it was free, she said we should look for a more respected charm school. I think she figured an expensive one would be better." Karen shrugged. "But I just knew I wanted to come here, so she let me stay and check it out."

My mouth was hanging wide open like a

jack-o'-lantern's. "How did you find it, Dana?"

She strapped her arms across her chest like maybe she wasn't going to tell us. Then she twisted her lips and said, "My dog, Pepper, got lost, and we put an ad in the paper in case anyone found him." She looked away. "I was really upset because I've had that dog since . . . since I was little. I put flyers up on every telephone pole in town."

"Let me guess. Miss Vernie found him, didn't she?"

She nodded. "When we came to pick him up, and I realized it was a charm school, I asked my daddy if I could come for lessons. Once he found out they were free, he said no problem. I hadn't even been thinking about going to charm school either until we found it."

The three of us stopped walking and stared at each other, not sure what to say. Finally Karen asked me, "What about you?"

My heart started beating fast just remembering that *tappity-tap-tap* noise when I found the sign. But it was too crazy to share with the girls. I kicked at a stone. "I was just walking down the road and saw the sign."

Karen wrinkled her nose. "That's not very interesting."

"Speaking of the school, maybe we should skip

the cattails for now and get back," Dana said. "We've been out here a long time."

We turned round in circles on the path, but we couldn't figure out which way to go. "Oh my gosh, you guys. We are so lost," Karen said.

"Let's just keep going this way." Dana pointed ahead. "Someone made this path, so it has to lead somewhere. We'll find our way."

We spent the next half hour walking down paths that turned us in circles and finally got us back to the main trail.

We plodded on toward Miss Vernie's house, tired from all that traipsing around. Before we stepped out of the woods, I set my hand on Dana's arm. "I had fun with you guys."

Those big yellow eyes of hers locked on mine. "That was cool, wasn't it?"

"Really cool," I said.

We walked up to the back porch, where Miss Vernie was arranging some flowers in a vase. "Hello, girls. You hungry?"

"Yeah," Karen said. "And you'll never believe what we found! That field with all the dandelions."

"Karen destroyed most of them," Dana said, flopping onto a chair.

Karen crossed her arms. "You guys were running

around too. And the seeds were going to fly anyway. We just helped them get where they were going a little sooner."

Miss Vernie smiled. "Can't say that I've ever seen your field."

"Really? It's right on the way to your pond," I said. "You have to come check it out. It's incredible!"

I took Miss Vernie by the hand and we led her down the path. But we made it all the way to the pond without spotting that golden glow off in the woods. I scratched my head, wondering how we'd missed it.

"Oh, look!" Miss Vernie said, pointing at the pond. "Lily pads! They weren't there before. How lovely!"

"Do we have to rip them up too?" Dana asked.

"Heavens, no. I'd hate to yank them out after they just showed up. We'll see what they have to say."

"What do you mean?" I asked.

"They must have shown up for a reason," Miss Vernie said. "Everything and everyone does."

That was good news, but I still wanted to get back to that field. "Let's head for the house. Maybe we'll see the path to the dandelions again." This time we walked real slow, but we still couldn't find it.

"Darn it," Karen said. "It was really neat. There were millions of fuzzy dandelions."

"You could've made a wish, Miss Vernie," Dana said.

"I don't need a dandelion to make a wish," Miss Vernie said. She set her hand on my shoulder. "And you don't need a wish to make your dreams come true."

My skin tingled under her touch, and her pale blue eyes twinkled like they held a million quiet secrets.

WHEN I GOT BACK TO GRANDMA'S, MAMA AND RUTHIE and Charlene were all in the living room, looking at a whole bunch of fancy dresses carefully laid out on the plastic-covered couch. Grandma stood next to them, smiling at the dresses like they were new grandbabies or something.

Mama waved me over. "Chip, come look at my old pageant dresses. Grandma saved them, can you believe it?"

Charlene held up a pale pink one in front of her, running her hands over the shiny material.

"You could use that for the talent portion," Grandma said. "Go try it on. Cecelia, you try one on too."

"It won't fit anymore," Mama said.

"Just zip it up the best you can," Grandma said.

Mama and Charlene looked at each other and

giggled. Then they both snatched up a dress and ran upstairs to change.

"Can I try one on?" I asked Grandma.

Grandma's eyes swept over me. "You're filthy."

"But . . ." I was about to argue, but then I stopped myself, remembering my promise. I wouldn't want to get one of Mama's beautiful gowns dirty and it probably wouldn't have fit anyway.

Sighing, I nodded. Besides, I wanted to wait until the pageant for my family to see me in my fancy dress. I was going to knock their socks off! That's what Daddy would've said.

Charlene and Mama ran down the stairs, the material of their dresses making a rustling sound. They stood in front of the mirror over Grandma's couch. Charlene wrinkled her nose. "It poufs out like it's from the sixties." She turned around to inspect herself.

"It *is* from the sixties," Mama said.

Charlene posed in front of the mirror. "I can't wear this for the pageant."

"You're right," Grandma said. "We're going to have to make you another dress for the talent competition if you want a real chance at winning. Something more sophisticated and sleek."

"What's my talent?" Ruthie asked.

"Being adorable," Grandma said, pinching Ruthie's cheek.

"There's no talent portion for you, Ruthie," Mama said, smoothing her hair while Ruthie put her hands on her hips and pouted. "You just have to get onstage and be your cute little self."

They were grinning at each other, while my stomach twisted. I wanted so bad to tell them I was joining too, but I was going to be patient for once and let this be a surprise, just like I had planned. I walked over and picked up one of the dresses. The material was white and silky, studded with rhinestones in the pattern of little roses. "You wore this, Mama?"

She nodded. "Grandma paid the best seamstress in the county to make these for me."

Grandma beamed. "You were exquisite in them. Those were good times, Cecelia. And I think we should continue our post-pageant tradition of a special five-course dinner afterward on my good china."

"A feast fit for a queen!" Mama and Grandma said at the same time, laughing.

"Beef Wellington, French onion soup, strawberry cheesecake—the works," Grandma said.

Mama clutched her hands in front of her and closed her eyes. "That was my favorite part of the pageants. Our celebrate-like-queens dinner."

My eyes widened. I loved cheesecake.

"And how about a new tradition?" Grandma asked. "Whoever brings home a crown gets to choose one of my dolls." She gestured to her doll cabinet.

Ruthie's eyes nearly popped out of her head and she ran over to the cabinet. Charlene squealed and said, "Really?" She stood beside Ruthie while they decided which doll they would choose.

"Mother, that's very kind of you," Mama said.

Grandma wrapped an arm around Mama's shoulder. "Well, this is an important milestone for the family, passing on the pageant torch to a new generation."

I looked over at the dolls, chewing on my bottom lip. Was there any chance I could win a crown? And even though I didn't want a china doll, I couldn't chase away the image of Grandma opening her cabinet and telling me to pick one out. But me in a crown? It seemed as likely as snow in July.

A FEW DAYS LATER, MISS VERNIE WAS ALL SMILES when we showed up after lunch. "Did you see that Saturday night, girls?" she asked us as we sat in the wicker chairs on her back deck. "It was amazing."

I knew what she was talking about. A black woman from some tiny island won Miss Universe. Grandma had sat there in front of the TV just blinking.

Karen nodded. "She looked just like a black Barbie doll."

Dana's grin was huge. "Did you see her dress, all shiny and gold? She looked like a queen." Her eyes were wide and bright. "It was like magic."

"I think we'll have some magical moments of our own at the Miss Dogwood pageant," Miss Vernie said.

"You do?" I asked.

Those secret-keeping eyes twinkled again. "Indeed, I do."

The three of us girls looked at each other, and I wondered if they felt the same rush of cool tingles on the back of their necks.

As the days flew by, I couldn't stop thinking about what Miss Vernie had said. Would the pageant be magical? I worked my hardest, practicing the baton, picking flowers, and pulling cattails. And Miss Vernie's gardens were thick and beautiful even though we hadn't had any rain. Grandma's flowers were all dried up. I didn't go back to the creek anymore, because I had pageant work to do.

I still had two charms to lose on my bracelet, but Karen and Dana each had three left, until Karen showed up breathless one morning, running up to us and shaking her wrist. "I lost my ballet slippers!"

We crowded around her on Miss Vernie's back porch to look. "What do you think you learned?" Dana asked.

Karen shrugged. "Maybe it's because I'm getting good at the baton?"

Dana glanced over at my wrist. "And you lost your flower."

I nodded. "A week or so ago."

"What did you learn, Brenda?" Miss Vernie asked.

I stared up at the clouds steaming across the sky. "People and ideas can grow on you. Just like a flower grows, you know?"

"Very good. Very good, indeed." Miss Vernie looked proud.

I leaned against the railing on her porch. "But I don't understand how the bracelet works, Miss Vernie. How does it know when to lose a charm? How does it know when you learn a lesson?"

She shrugged. "How is it that *you* know?"

I studied my bracelet. I wasn't sure, but I did know I had two charms left and no idea what I still had to learn.

AFTER OUR USUAL MORNING ROUTINE, WE GATHERED for lunch. Karen ran her hand along her cheek. "My skin really does look good after using that clay. See?"

She tilted her chin toward us. "My zits are clearing up. Better than Clearasil."

"You do look lovely." Miss Vernie nodded.

Then Karen stood up. She pulled on the waist of her shorts. "I've lost some weight too." She was smiling as she plopped back in her seat and pushed her unfinished plate away. "I even told my stepfather about it when he called me porky."

"He called you porky?" I asked.

"No, but he said I didn't need second helpings of dessert," she said. "That's when I showed him my loose shorts."

"Sounds like you're standing on your own two feet," Miss Vernie said with a smile.

"Your two feet in two *ballet slippers*," I offered.

Karen's eyes widened. "You think that's what I learned? I thought I learned something about beauty, but we already lost the mirror. Maybe you're right." She looked off for a while. "My skin looks as nice as yours in that picture on your piano, Miss Vernie. The one where you look like a movie star."

Our gazes went to the French doors where you could see her pictures on the big baby grand piano.

"So who is that man in the picture next to you?" Dana asked, which was very strange, because she had yelled at us for asking before.

The man stared out from underneath an army cap. He had Miss Vernie's thin nose and pouty lips.

Miss Vernie took a deep breath. "That's my Charlie."

We chewed silently, waiting for more of an explanation. Was he her son? A brother? A boyfriend? But she said nothing.

"What happened to him?" Karen asked.

I kicked her under the table.

"Hey," she yelped, rubbing her leg.

We were all quiet for a while until Miss Vernie finally raised her head. But her eyes were still fixed on the table. "I don't know. I don't know what happened to Charlie. I don't know where he is."

I opened my mouth to ask how that could be, but then snapped it shut. I figured Miss Vernie would tell us if she wanted to.

Even Karen knew enough not to say anything.

Dana looked at Miss Vernie with big, sad eyes. "I'm sure Miss Vernie would appreciate a break from the three of us so she can have some quiet time to herself. Let's go back to the pond."

We hadn't worked there in a few days, and the idea snapped us out of our funk.

"Okay," I said, trying not to sound too excited.

"Yes!" Karen shouted. "More mud. Can we have

more plastic containers, please?"

Miss Vernie hurried to the kitchen, back to her usual smiling self.

It took a little while to get into our groove but we worked through the afternoon, silent and smooth like a machine. After a few hours, we'd cleared another twenty feet. We had finished half the pond. It was hard work in the hot sun, but it felt good. We collapsed on the shore, dangling our feet in the water. I grabbed another handful of mud to smear on my face.

"Good idea," Karen said.

I was hoping Dana would pick some up too, so we could all be the same. But she just closed her eyes and basked in the sun, twining a piece of marsh grass around her finger. "I've still got three charms left."

"Guess you've got a lot to learn," I said.

"You don't know anything about me," she said quietly.

"But I'd like to."

Dana thought about this for a moment and nodded. Then she got up and packed her things. "I've got a lot of chores to do at home. See you guys tomorrow."

We watched her walk away.

Karen examined her bracelet. "I sure hope these charms teach us something that'll help us at the pageant. It's getting close."

She was right. Even after all this time at Miss Vernie's, I knew nothing about getting onstage and acting like a beauty queen. And how was ripping cattails out of a pond going to help? If this pageant didn't bring me closer to my family, I didn't know what would. Chip was gone and I wasn't sure who I was becoming.

chapter fourteen

Miss Vernie set us to work weeding another garden the next morning. We were busy pulling out clover and thick, creeping ivy that must have popped up overnight. We had just cleared out that garden two days before. Now that I wanted to surprise my family and show them I was a pageant girl too, I wanted real lessons that would help me. But I had promised to do whatever she asked back when I joined the school, so it felt wrong to grumble about it.

After working for a while, Miss Vernie checked on us. "Girls, we need to go back into town today. I have to buy some supplies and I'd like to give you a treat for your hard work."

We stopped weeding. The tips of my fingers were stained green.

"What kind of treat?" Karen asked. "Ice cream?" She licked her lips.

"I'm going to drop you off at the movie show while I do my errands."

"Cool! *Star Wars* is playing. Everyone says it's amazing. I haven't seen it yet, have you?" Karen asked me.

"No," I said. I hadn't been to the movies in months, and I didn't want to see some spaceship movie. But *Star Wars* was playing at the matinee, so that was our movie.

Miss Vernie paid the dollar and fifty cents for our tickets and bought us popcorn and sodas too. She looked at her watch. "I'll meet you here in two hours. Have a wonderful time." She waved good-bye and we handed our tickets to the usher.

We walked into the cool, dark theater. That in itself was a nice treat from the steamy day. I never imagined summer in the South would be so hot. We walked down the aisle, looking for a seat. There were plenty to choose from on a Tuesday afternoon.

"Dana, what are you doing, girl? Where you been this summer?" Two black girls stood up from their seats and looked at her.

She bent her head to take a long drink from her straw. "I've been busy." She didn't look at them.

"Doing what? Babysitting for some white family?" one of the girls asked with a little laugh.

Dana didn't say anything.

The other girl patted the seat next to her. "Sit by us. Those girls are big enough to take care of themselves."

Dana's eyes flashed over at us and then back at the girls. "Naw, I'm good. I'll see you guys later." And she led us down the aisle away from the girls' whispers.

"It's okay if you want to sit with your friends," Karen said quietly, eating her popcorn one piece at a time.

"Yeah, it's dark. We wouldn't even know you were gone."

Dana looked down her nose at me. "You don't want me sitting with you?" Her amber eyes glowed in the dim theater.

If there was a wrong thing to say to her, it always seemed to land in my mouth, just like a hornet lands on your Popsicle right when you set it down. "No, I just don't want you to feel like you have to sit with us if you'd rather sit with your friends."

"I said I'm fine where I am."

We were quiet then, waiting for the movie. I

dropped my box of popcorn when *Star Wars* started—with that music and those stars shooting past me like I was out there in space too. The three of us laughed and cringed and dropped our jaws all at the same places. Karen offered me some of her popcorn and we drained our big sodas. We stood up and cheered when Luke blew up the Death Star and we kept clapping after the movie ended.

"That was great," Karen said as we stayed in our seats, watching the credits roll. I didn't want to leave. I closed my eyes and imagined myself flying through the stars at light speed. Then I frowned, remembering the night at the dinner table when I'd told Grandma what Miss Vernie had said about women joining the space program. Grandma got all mad.

"Women don't have the same opportunities as men," she'd said. "Women will never fly in space." And that had been the end of the conversation

"What's wrong?" Karen asked, noticing my frown.

"It was a cool movie," I said. "But why didn't Princess Leia get to fly the ship or blow anything up? Most of the time they were just rescuing her."

"But she was a princess. And she was funny. Bossy too. Man, Luke and Han are such foxes," Karen said with a sigh. "Of course she was waiting around for them to rescue her. That's what I would do."

"Come on, Miss Vernie's waiting for us," Dana said. We got up and crunched across spilled popcorn and sticky soda.

Miss Vernie clutched a few bags and scanned the lobby. She smiled when she spotted us exiting the theater doors. "How was it, girls? Did you have a good time together?"

"It was great!" Karen pumped her arm in the air.

"Real nice, ma'am. Thank you," said Dana.

"Hey! You lost a charm." I pointed to Dana's bracelet.

"The ballet slippers," Karen said. "What did you learn? Wait, let's think." Karen tapped a finger against her chin. "You had to do a little tap dancing when your friends wanted you to sit with them." Karen shuffled her feet in a quick dance.

"What's this?" Miss Vernie asked.

"Some of Dana's friends thought she should be sitting with them instead of us," Karen said.

"Oh, so what did you do, dear?"

"I sat with my charm school friends," Dana said, a tiny smile curling up the corners of her lips.

"Sounds like you stood up for what you believe in. On your own two feet, if you will." Miss Vernie winked at Dana.

Dana looked up at Miss Vernie and smiled.

Was that what would happen for me too?

Karen chattered on about the movie as we walked toward Miss Vernie's car. "It was the best movie ever! Well, Chip didn't like that Princess Leia didn't get to drive any of the spaceships. But it's not like there are any girl astronauts. That's for boys," Karen said.

I jabbed Karen with my elbow. "Shhh!" I hissed. What a blabbermouth. That should be her talent for Junior Miss Dogwood.

"Why wouldn't a woman fly a spaceship?" Miss Vernie asked as we loaded ourselves into her car. "I just read in the paper that they're accepting applications at NASA for the space shuttle program. Remember how I told you they were testing it? I bet there'll be women in that class."

"No way," Karen said, shaking her head.

"Maybe someday our Chip will be the first-ever female astronaut." Miss Vernie studied me in the rearview mirror. Her bony fingers gripped the steering wheel.

"I couldn't do something like that," I said. But a little voice whispered in my head, *Then why do you think you can be in the pageant?* I shook my head to get rid of the thought. "What did you do while we were at the movies?"

"I had to get some new makeup for my contestants."

I scrunched my nose because I had never worn makeup before, but then I reminded myself that I'd never covered my face in mud before either, and that had been fine.

We drove home the rest of the way in silence while my mind twirled with images of speeding stars and sparkly tiaras.

chapter fifteen

WHEN I WALKED THROUGH OUR FRONT DOOR, I COULD see Grandma upstairs, walking past the off-limits room. Inspired by the adventures in the movie, I decided I would try to get back in there soon. But I was never alone in the house. Did I dare do it again while everyone was sleeping? Probably not. Grandma had really good hearing for an old lady.

"You received some correspondence today," Grandma said as she walked down the stairs.

"What?"

"You got mail, little sis," Charlene said, leaning over the railing. "I think it's from your boyfriend," she sang.

"He's not my boyfriend," I grumbled. But why was I blushing?

Grandma walked over and handed me a letter. It was from Billy. I recognized his handwriting. I ran to my room to read it in private, ignoring Charlene's giggles as I dashed past her.

I jumped on the bed and turned Deady Freddy around so he couldn't see the letter. Then I tore open the thick envelope.

Dear Chip,

Things are soooooo boring here. It's no fun playing the Coolest Thing Ever when there's no one to show your stuff to. Thanks for the rock. Awesome! It's in my crayfish tank. I found an albino crayfish that might actually be cooler than your baby turtle. Do you still have him?

I'm sorry to hear you don't like it down there. I saw Star Wars—*did you see it? It was so cool! I got you some PopRocks at the movies, since they're your favorite, and stuck them in the envelope. Hope they didn't get crushed.*

Well, please come back and visit sometime.

Your pal,

Billy

I rolled over onto my stomach and stared out the window. It was so strange not having a friend I could just run outside and play with. Dana had called me and Karen her charm school friends today, but it wasn't the same as with Billy. I missed skipping stones across the pond and riding bikes. I couldn't remember ever feeling sad like this back home before Daddy died. I felt like a wilted flower down here in North Carolina, and Billy's letter only reminded me how much had changed. How much I had changed.

"WHO WANTS TO GO INTO TOWN FOR ICE CREAM?" Grandma asked after dinner.

"Me! Me! Me!" hollered Ruthie, jumping up and down like a puppy.

Charlene held her hand over her stomach. "I'm stuffed. But I'll come and have one maraschino cherry. That only has fifteen calories."

I was pouring the PopRocks onto my tongue, seeing how long it would take for them to run out of pop. I wondered if they'd do the same thing on ice cream. It would be a worthwhile experiment even if it did mean a trip in Grandma's stuffy car.

"Brenda, I thought I told you not to eat those. Children across America are being rushed to emergency rooms every day because that candy is blowing

holes in their stomachs. Where did you get that?"
Mama asked.

"Her boyfriend," Charlene teased.

"Not true!"

"Brenda, did you hear from Billy? How is he?"
Mama asked.

"Great. I sure do miss him." Billy would've known
how to get back in Grandma's room. I froze. Grandma
was going to town for ice cream. The house would be
empty. This was my chance. I rubbed my stomach.

"I'm full too. I'm going to skip the ice cream. I'll
be upstairs."

"Suit yourself," Grandma said, plucking her keys
from the key rack.

As they filed out the door, my heart pounded.
They'd all be gone for at least an hour, and that was
plenty of time for investigating the off-limits room—
I wanted to look at all the pictures and see what
was inside that covered-up cabinet. I needed to learn
some of Grandma's secrets and I'd bet anything that's
where they were. Too bad Billy wasn't there to act as
a lookout.

I waited for the car to pull out of the driveway.
Then I ran upstairs. My fingers trembled as I snatched
another bobby pin out of the drawer in the bathroom.

I held it in my palm, giving myself one last chance to decide not to do it. But I wasn't doing it to be sneaky. I was doing it to know Grandma better, and that was all part of keeping my promise to Mama. I blew out a breath. It sure sounded good, but it didn't feel good. Before I could change my mind, I stuck the pin in the lock and opened the door.

The room looked exactly like it did the last time I had been in there. It was still dim, but I wasn't brave enough to flip a light on. I scanned the walls for those animal pictures again. There were dozens of framed photos tacked up on the wall.

I stopped in front of one picture that looked just like Ruthie. I blew off the dust. This little Ruthie-Girl smiled up at the camera with lots of baby bunnies at her feet. In another picture that same little girl held onto a great big fluffy kitty. Then the girl stood with a man and a woman in front of an old truck that had DAVIDSON ANIMAL HUSBANDRY printed on its side.

I brushed off another dusty picture of the little girl and froze. There was something scribbled in pencil underneath a picture of her on a pony. I squinted so I could read it better. *Nancy riding Ginger, 1926*, it read.

Grandma's name was Nancy. That little Ruthie-Girl was Grandma. That little Ruthie-Girl with all those animals! Grandma—who hates animals. I spotted another picture, with Grandma holding a ribbon tied around a goat's neck. And that wasn't the only picture of Grandma with animals. Live animals—not dead, stuffed ones like downstairs.

I moved a few boxes out of the way so I could get to the cabinet. I had to know why it was all covered up. Taking a deep breath, I pulled the blanket to the side.

"That's it?" I whispered to myself.

The cabinet was like the ones in the living room with the lit-up dolls, but this one had rows of carved wooden animals. There was a whole shelf of animals you'd see on a farm. Another one had animals from the jungle. Cats had their own shelf and dogs filled two. Why was she covering these up?

I didn't have too much time to be stunned because I heard a car door slam. They hadn't been gone an hour. More like a few minutes. I turned to leave, but the blanket fell down.

"Shoot!" I said. I wouldn't be able to get that back on. I locked the door and closed it behind me just as they were walking up the sidewalk.

"I can't believe I forgot my pocketbook. You girls help me find it, all right?" I heard Grandma say.

I headed for the stairs, but Grandma looked up, and saw me in front of the off-limits room. I felt so guilty I couldn't help but stare at the shiny wood floor.

Grandma dashed up those stairs. Then Mama followed her, and Charlene and Ruthie tore after them. I thought about running out the front door, but I stood frozen in the same spot. Grandma went right to the door and twisted the knob. It opened.

Rats. I'd forgotten to lock it. Not that it mattered. She knew just from looking at me that I'd gone in. I thought I might throw up.

Grandma stood outside the room, turning red and shaking. She was a firework waiting for the flame to race down the wick so she could explode.

And she did. "Brenda Anderson, I made it clear that you were not to go in this room. But you went in anyway. And now you've gone in again! You just don't listen. I ought to . . ." But Grandma was so upset she couldn't even think of what horrible thing she ought to do to me.

"What are all those pictures with the animals?" My brain worked in reverse, opening my mouth by mistake when it should be clamped shut. "I saw one of you with a horse. And one with a goat. I thought you hated animals. You must have a hundred animal statues in that cabinet."

Mama flashed me a scary look. "Brenda, you keep quiet and tell Grandma you're sorry."

But Grandma held out her hand. "No, no, Cecelia. Since Brenda is so interested, Brenda should know. She should know life isn't always about what *you* want or what *you* like."

Mama closed her eyes and dropped her chin to her chest. Ruthie grabbed on to her leg.

"Grandma, I'm sorry . . . I—"

She cut me off. "You want to know about that goat in the picture? I'll tell you about that goat. I grew up during the Great Depression," Grandma said, walking down the hall with her hands behind her back. "Do they teach you about that at school? Food was scarce. Money too. Sometimes we got only one meal a day." She turned around to look at me, and held up one finger. "No ice cream sundaes for us."

We all stood there. I wished she had just sent me to my room.

Grandma started pacing again. Her voice was deep and low. "My father was the vet in town. But no one else had any money either. He got paid with scraps of material or vegetables, sometimes a chicken. Once a baby goat." Grandma stopped to take a deep breath. Her voice was running out of hate. "I thought Daddy had brought it home for my birthday. I thought that baby goat was going to be my pet. But it wasn't." Now she almost sounded like she was a little girl again. "A few months later when that goat got fat, it became dinner." She stopped to take a shaky breath "And when I had to marry your grandfather, animals didn't fit in my life anymore."

I think she forgot we were there, because her eyes were fixed on something in the room. After a few minutes, she walked downstairs. The back door slammed.

We were all quiet.

Finally I looked at Mama and went back into the open room, dark and dusty like a mummy's tomb that had just been opened. Charlene and Ruthie followed me. We walked around slowly, looking at all the pictures, not even talking.

"That's me!" Ruthie said, jumping up and pointing to the photo of Grandma on the pony. She stood on her tippy-toes, trying to get a better look.

"That's Grandma, honey," Mama said.

I stared at another picture of Grandma; this time she was holding a chicken. "Seems like she liked animals a long time ago," I said. "So why not now?"

Mama sank down on a big orange couch. She rested her head in her hands and then looked up. "Grandma did love animals. She went out with her daddy on his vet calls. She wanted to be an animal doctor like him one day." Mama forced a wobbly smile. "She was such a daddy's girl, always working out in the barn with him."

I squeezed my hands around my ribs. "She was kind of like a tomboy? Like me?" My heart kicked up a notch.

Mama nodded. "Yes, she was. She doesn't talk about it now, but my grandma Davidson would tell me stories. Your grandma was always stubborn. Everyone laughed when she told them her dreams because she was a girl and girls weren't vets. But she didn't care—she was going to do it."

I studied the picture. "Why didn't she become one?"

Mama pulled a blanket over her lap and rubbed the fringe between her fingers. "It was a different world back then. And times were tough, like Grandma said. Grandma was a beautiful girl. Just like you all." She blew out a long breath, ruffling her bangs. "Her mama said she should forget about being a vet and find herself a rich husband."

Charlene took a picture off the wall to look at it closer. "And did she?"

Mama shook her head. "Not right away. When she was seventeen, her mother made her quit showing the farm animals at the fair and join the beauty pageant instead. She won the county fair title and went on to the state competition. She won the state title the next year when she was eighteen. She thought she could use the prize money toward school, toward being a vet." Mama sighed.

"So what happened?" Charlene asked.

"Her daddy couldn't keep up with the bills anymore. And the bank was ready to take his house and his business. This happened to a lot of people during the depression. It was a very scary time." Mama stared off at nothing.

"Did they lose the house and everything?" I asked.

Mama gave me a tight smile and shook her head. "The man who owned the bank said he'd be interested in investing in the business. But only if he was related to the family."

"Was he?" Charlene cocked her head.

"Once he married Grandma he was."

The polished tips of Charlene's fingers flew to her mouth. "Grandma had to marry the banker? You mean Grandpa? Did she love him?" Her lips turned down in a horrified frown.

Mama shrugged. "She didn't really know him. And as you can see in the pictures, he was much older. But her marriage saved the family."

"Grandma told you this?" Charlene asked.

Mama laughed. "No, my grandma Davidson did, before she died." Mama shivered and pulled the blanket around her. "My mother wouldn't admit her life wasn't what she wanted. And she didn't want to upset her father and let him know she wasn't happy."

"Why didn't she just work with her daddy and be a vet after she got married?" I sat down in a chair across from Mama, feeling a little shaky. I actually felt bad for Grandma.

"Your grandpa wouldn't allow that. He had this big house for her to take care of. And he wanted to start a family."

I stared at the pictures of little Ruthie-Grandma and all those animals. "Why didn't she just get a whole bunch of pets? That's what I would've done."

"Grandpa thought animals were only good for being hunted and for eating."

"But still, not even a dog or a cat?"

Mama sighed. "Oh, Chip. You ask more questions than a newspaper reporter. Sometimes when you lose something you love, it's better not to think of it at all." Her voice got quiet. "It just hurts so darn much, you push it right out of your mind so you don't think about what's gone." She twisted her fingers in her lap and spun her wedding ring around and around on her finger. "That's what Grandma did with animals and those dreams of hers. Tucked 'em away."

I swallowed hard and watched to see if Mama was going to cry. But she stood up. "Let's go, girls."

I stopped and looked back in the room. "Wait. That explains why she doesn't like animals, but why didn't she like Daddy?"

Charlene glared at me. "Hush, Chip!"

"It's Brenda," I protested. "I'm Brenda, now."

Charlene rolled her eyes. "Chip suits you way more than Brenda."

Mama ran a hand through her hair and looked at the floor, not even paying attention to our squabbling. "Grandma didn't like Daddy because she had big dreams for me. All the big dreams she had wanted for herself." She squeezed her eyes shut and shook her head, like she was trying to shake an idea away. "And when I got married so young, she blamed your daddy. But we were getting ready for Charlene," she said slowly, opening her eyes, "and we wanted to get married real fast." She was looking at Charlene while she said this.

Charlene's eyes got real wide. "What? You never told me."

Mama reached her hand out toward her. "Charlene—"

"I'll be in my room." She pushed her way out the door to leave.

Mama stood, frozen, and bit her knuckle.

I tugged on Mama's shirt. "Why is she so upset? Grandma likes her. If you got married getting ready for Charlene, shouldn't she be mad at Charlene instead of me?" I asked.

Mama rubbed her eyes. "She's not mad at you, Brenda. She's hard on you because you are just like your father. And it was easier to be angry with him than it was with me. And maybe she sees some of herself in you. The way she used to be when she was little. Maybe it reminds her of everything she gave up."

I stomped my foot. "It's not fair. I didn't do anything. I finally have a grandma and she is nothing at all like a grandma should be."

Mama rubbed my back. "You've gotta love people for who they are, even if they aren't what you were hoping for."

I narrowed my eyes. "Doesn't seem like Grandma knows that."

She looked at me like she was going to say something. Then she sighed. "I have to go check on Charlene."

Ruthie chased after Mama, and I sank down

onto the stair, wishing I'd just gone out for ice cream instead of unlocking all this trouble.

HALF AN HOUR LATER, GRANDMA CAME BACK INSIDE and went into her bedroom.

She didn't come out of her room for the rest of the night. Mama went out to buy us ice cream from the grocery store, and we ate it in front of the TV in the family room. No one said much, and it was all my fault.

I stirred the ice cream in my bowl until it turned into soup. I wished I hadn't snooped and learned the truth about all those pictures. Because now I felt mad at her *and* sorry for her. And those two feelings were hard to feel at the same time.

I headed for bed early, and Charlene caught up to me. She grabbed my arm. "You are ruining everything. Stop butting heads with Grandma. Are you trying to make things worse? It's only upsetting Mama," she hissed.

"I'm trying to fit in, Charlene."

"Try harder." She let go of me and marched back downstairs.

And how was I supposed to do that? I crawled into bed and kept thinking about the pictures and those carved animals. I set Deady Freddy next to me in bed and stared at the ceiling. "Grandma doesn't like me because I remind her of the way she used to be," I whispered to Freddy. "Learning more about Grandma hadn't helped at all." I stroked his feathers as I lay there, running things through my head. My only chance to get along with Grandma was to show her that I was like her now. I had to do whatever it took to be a good beauty queen. I imagined eating cheesecake off fancy plates and all of us girls hanging our dresses with Mama's old gowns in Grandma's closet. This had to work.

chapter sixteen

THE NEXT MORNING, I FOUND MISS VERNIE INSIDE AT her dining room table with Dana and Karen.

"Miss Vernie, you need to put a whole bunch of makeup on me and make me look totally different. Like a beauty queen."

"Looking totally different isn't the key, Brenda. You want to be yourself onstage." Miss Vernie pinched together a pair of tweezers as she and Karen sat at her dining room table sorting through her makeup supplies.

No, I don't, I thought. I needed a whole new look. I needed to be Brand-New Brenda.

"You don't seem like the makeup type," Dana said.

"Well, I'm going to be."

"Me too. I love makeup," Karen said, inspecting the different colors of eye shadow laid out in front of her.

Miss Vernie patted the chair next to her. "Sit down, Brenda. Just a few touches here and there will do the trick." A feathery brush tickled my eyelids. Then she coated my eyelashes with mascara.

"Part your lips," Miss Vernie said.

I did, and she slicked on a coat of lipstick. I smacked my lips together. "Yuck, it tastes waxy. And my eyes feel itchy."

"You're just not used to it." Miss Vernie handed me a mirror. "What do you think?"

I looked at myself. "I don't look that different."

"Like I said, it's just a touch of makeup to bring out the beauty that's already there."

"But I thought I'd look totally different." I tracked my fingers over the pink mark on my cheek. "And shouldn't we cover this up? It's embarrassing."

Miss Vernie set down a tube of lipstick. "We can if that makes you feel more comfortable, Brenda."

"It will."

"Then I'll bring foundation for you on the day of

the pageant." Miss Vernie smoothed the back of my head.

"What do you think we should do with our hair?" Karen asked, flipping through a magazine.

"Most girls wear it down. But you wear it however you like. I've said it before: the key is being yourself."

Silently I disagreed.

"This is my only look." Dana patted her hair in the mirror.

"And it's beautiful on you," Miss Vernie told her.

"I guess I'll wear my hair down," Karen said. "And I'm going to use some lemon juice so it'll be nice and bright. Mom's going to take me to the salon for a new cut. What about you, Brenda?"

I shrugged. "Maybe I'll put it in a braid."

Karen grabbed my shoulders. "No way. You need a style—not just straight—if you want to win."

I shoved my hands in my pockets. "I don't have enough money left."

"I'll cut it for you. One of my *Teen Beat* magazines had exact instructions on how to cut your hair just like Farrah Fawcett from *Charlie's Angels* does, with the big feather flips. I've practiced on my dolls. I'll bring the magazine and some scissors tomorrow. Please?" She folded her hands like she was begging.

"Okay." Charlene had her hair cut with big feather

flips. Maybe having the same haircut as a TV star could help Brand-New Brenda be a beauty queen.

THE NEXT MORNING, I MET KAREN AND DANA EARLY on Miss Vernie's back porch. Karen draped a towel around my shoulders, then flipped open her magazine. "Okay, first I'm supposed to pull it up and run my fingers through it." She fluffed my hair and pulled it in all sorts of directions. Dana was snickering at the table, reading her magazine.

Karen held the scissors in the air and finally made her first snip at the back of my head. A thick clump of my honey-colored hair fluttered to the floor.

"Are you sure this is going to work?" I asked. I looked for Miss Vernie to speak up, but she was outside in her garden. So I closed my eyes and hoped for the best. The metal blades sliced against each other as Karen cut another section. Karen's breath caught.

Dana coughed and her chair scraped along the floor, and I opened my eyes and saw her hand fly to her mouth. "It'll grow back," Dana whispered.

I reached up to touch my hair. I grabbed a mirror.

"It looks good," Karen said, trying to convince us both.

"This does not look like the magazine." My voice was shaky. The sides were uneven and did not fold back into feathery wings. It just looked chopped up.

Karen put her hand on her hip. "Well, of course not. Not yet. We need to use a curling iron. I brought one. Let's go to the bathroom and plug it in."

We went inside. We usually used Miss Vernie's little bathroom off her kitchen, but that one didn't have an outlet. This time, we walked past her bedroom to the big bathroom with a counter and giant mirror. "Should we ask first?" I said, not daring to look in the mirror.

"Nah, she knows we're working on your hair. She won't mind if we're in here." Karen tapped her fingers against the metal barrel of the curling iron, waiting for it to heat up. "There. Now let's see what we can do."

She closed the pink toilet lid and pushed me down on it. Then she started sliding sections of hair under the clamp of the barrel, leaving big sausage curls behind.

Dana's eyes grew wide. "I don't know much about white girls' hair, but that don't look right." She left the bathroom.

Karen chewed on her lip. She did that a lot now that she wasn't eating as much. She put in a few more curls while I gripped the cold toilet seat, pressing my knees together.

Dana came back holding a crown.

"What is that?" Karen asked, setting down the curling iron.

"It's a beauty pageant crown," I whispered. I stood up and took it from Dana. I set it on my head. Even with the horrible haircut I could imagine myself walking and waving with a sparkly crown on my head. Junior Miss Dogwood, 1977. I closed my eyes and smiled.

"Miss Vernie was Miss North Carolina 1939!" Dana said.

My eyes flew open. "What? 1939? No, she wasn't. My grandma was."

"But look at this." Dana pulled a photo from behind her back of a much younger Miss Vernie with the Miss North Carolina 1939 sash across her chest and the crown on her head. We stood there examining it. Karen scratched her head.

"I thought it had gotten a little quiet in here."

We all jumped, and the crown toppled off my head. Miss Vernie stood in the doorway with a flat look in her eyes and tight lips. I almost didn't recognize her.

"I'm sorry." I wanted to disappear. I bent down to pick up the crown and handed it to her.

"I noticed this stuff in your bedroom when we

came in to use your bathroom for curling Brenda's hair," Dana said, staring at the black and white tiles on the floor.

"Why didn't you tell us you were Miss North Carolina 1939?" Karen asked.

"My grandma said she was Miss North Carolina 1939." I looked up into her eyes, remembering what Grandma said about Miss Vernie going daft. I wasn't totally sure what that meant, but I knew it wasn't good.

She let out her breath. "It's all very complicated. But I did win." She fiddled with a button on her dress.

"But my grandma said she won."

Miss Vernie nodded. "She took over the title for me. My sister died three weeks after I won the crown. I had to give it up." Her hands were shaking.

"Oh, no!" Karen covered her mouth with her hands.

Tears pricked my eyes. Miss Vernie cleared her throat. "So I stepped down. And Brenda's grandmother, the first runner-up, was named Miss North Carolina 1939."

My throat tightened. "Grandma didn't tell me that part."

We stood silently for a moment. The only thing I could hear was a couple of squirrels chattering outside the window.

"That's real sad about your sister," Dana said. "But why was that a reason to drop out?"

"Dana!" I surprised myself by shouting at her. "Your own mama died! You should know you just might feel like you'll never breathe again. That you might never find your smile again. How could Miss Vernie go around smiling and waving like a beauty queen when something so awful happened? I understand, Miss Vernie, I really do." I caught a glimpse of my head bobbing in the mirror with those huge curls bouncing.

Dana clutched her hands behind her back. "I didn't say my mama died for sure. I said I think she's dead."

"How could you not know if your mama's dead or not?" I asked.

She lowered her voice. "Because she left when I was five and I never heard from her again." Dana studied the floor some more. "She must have died if she didn't come back."

We were all quiet again. Miss Vernie took the crown from the counter. "I had to resign," she said softly, "because my sister and her husband were killed in a car crash. My mother was gone, so it was just me and my father left to take care of their son. It was either that or an orphanage, and I wasn't going to let that happen. Father had to work, and I couldn't very well go touring across the state with a baby. It wouldn't have seemed proper. The organizers felt bad about it and let me keep the crown at least, if not the title."

We all stood there staring at our toes until Miss Vernie said, "Let's comb your hair out and see what we have." She pulled a pink brush out of a drawer and smoothed out my bushy, uneven hair.

All three of them gawked at me.

"Well . . . ," Dana started to say something, but then she closed her mouth.

"I don't care. I've never cared what my hair looked like." Only now I did. I really did.

Karen covered her eyes. "I'm so sorry! I followed the directions in my magazine. I don't know what happened."

Miss Vernie patted my hand. "Don't fret, Brenda. We can take you to town and get this fixed up at the salon. I'll even pay for it. I shouldn't have left you alone to do this."

"Thanks," I said.

"Can we go work in the pond?" Karen sounded desperate.

Miss Vernie nodded, and we ran off, leaving her alone, holding her crown.

chapter seventeen

When I got home, I snuck into the house and put on a baseball cap. I didn't want anyone to see my hair until it was fixed. How would I explain that one? Nobody really paid me much attention, though. My sisters sat at the kitchen table sorting through Mama's makeup and looking at lipstick shades.

"I get to wear makeup?" Ruthie asked.

"A little bit, sugar," Mama said, squeezing Ruthie's cheek. Ruthie clapped and bounced in her seat.

I stared at the back of Grandma's head as she stood cooking over the stove. I wanted to tell her I knew her real secret. Not the sad ones hidden in her off-limits room. The bad one. The sneaky one. That she didn't win Miss North Carolina. That she got it by mistake. Because of a horrible accident. And all this time, she'd been pretending. Lying.

Even though I was mostly angry, my throat felt thick and I wanted to cry. Grandma had tricked us. She tricked us all and made us think she was something she wasn't. A little thought crept into my head. "Isn't that what you're trying to do? Trick them into thinking you're Brand-New Brenda the Beauty Queen?" I chased that idea away like a pesky fly. I wasn't trying to trick anyone. I was *trying* to be someone new. But Grandma fooled us. She told us all she was a winner when she wasn't.

LATER I FIXED A NASTY STARE AT HER ACROSS THE DIN-ner table and ignored the way she glared at my baseball cap. "So, Grandma, what was it like when you won the crown? When you were onstage and they put it on your head?" I poked some peas around my plate. I hated peas.

"Yes, tell us. Did you cry?" Charlene asked, settling her chin in her hand.

Mama shifted in her seat. "Mother, we need to buy some more thread for Charlene's gown. Shall we go to town tomorrow?"

"Yes, yes, of course," she said.

"But tell us about winning the crown," I said. "About that very night."

I snuck a fresh look at Grandma. The side of her mouth curled down. "It's so hard to remember the exact moment. I didn't cry. I was just so happy. So proud."

"But were you nervous? With all the people in the audience watching when they announced your name that very night?" I asked.

"No. Not at all. You have to be confident onstage."

"Weren't you at all nervous you were going to lose?"

Grandma dropped her fork on the plate. "Why all these questions? It's not like *you* need to worry about what it's like to win a crown, Brenda. You're not a pageant girl."

I adjusted my baseball cap and shifted in my seat, pressing my lips together so I wouldn't blurt out my secret: I was going to be a pageant girl too. It was going to be so fun to see Grandma's surprised face when she saw me onstage.

THE NEXT DAY, I KEPT MY HEAD DOWN AS WE WALKED along the sidewalk into BeBe's salon. BeBe was friends with Miss Vernie and, hopefully, a hair genius. She just had to help me.

"Brenda?" Mama was standing right in front of me with a little bag from Woolworth's. I forgot my family was coming into town for thread!

I looked up. Mama rushed forward and ran her hand along my hair. "What happened? Who did this to you?" She looked at our group and her eyes landed on Dana.

Dana raised her eyebrows and dropped her chin. She planted a fist on her hip.

Don't say anything, Mama, I thought. *Don't.* She might ruin everything with just a few sharp words. "My friends and I tried cutting it. At charm school."

Mama looked at Miss Vernie. "Miss Vernie, I haven't seen you in years. Chip told me about your school, but I didn't think she was going there anymore."

My mouth opened and closed. "I am. I like it there. And I'm learning a lot."

"Brenda is doing a fine job," Miss Vernie said.

"Wait. Does this mean you're joining the pageant?" Mama asked, looking confused.

Suddenly the crack in the sidewalk seemed real interesting. "Yes, Mama. It was supposed to be a surprise. That's why I didn't tell you I was going to the school."

Grandma stepped forward, holding her purse in front of her. "Vernie, these girls are in your charm school?"

"Hello, Nancy. Yes, this is Karen and Dana. We're in town to make a few adjustments to Brenda's hair." Miss Vernie put on a big smile.

"Brenda," Charlene said, "I told you, you're not cut out for this pageant stuff. It's not like just anybody can do it." Then she looked right at Dana.

"Vernie, are you helping this girl for some Negro pageant?" Grandma asked.

"Grandma!" I snarled through my teeth.

"No, Dana is entering the Miss Dogwood pageant too." Miss Vernie stood behind Dana and set her hands on her shoulders.

"Juniors?" Charlene asked, taking in Dana, spending a lot of time staring at her Afro.

"No. I'm fifteen." Dana's eyes were as tight as her lips.

Mama put her hand on her throat. "But, surely you know . . ." Her voice trailed off.

"Just what kind of school are you running?" Grandma asked.

Miss Vernie raised her chin. "It's a school where the girls learn exactly what they need."

Grandma shook her head and sighed. "Brenda,

come with us. We'll take you to my salon and fix this mess on your head. We'll set you straight for the pageant best we can. But who knows what damage's been done. If you intended to join the pageant, you should have been working with me all along. But what should I expect from a sneak and a liar."

"I said I wanted to surprise you all."

Mama held out her hand, waiting for me. "Brenda, come." Mama was using her disappointed voice. She should have been clapping her hands together, thrilled with the news. But she wasn't excited at all that I was trying to be like her. Where was Mama's smile? I thought my heart might drop right out of my chest.

"Mama, let her be. She's been going to a charm school instead of working with us. Let's see what she can do on her own. Besides, there is so much to do for me and Ruthie. There's no way we can help her too," Charlene said, jerking her thumb my way.

Even Ruthie was wrinkling her nose. The four of them stood across from me.

I slid my fingers in my pockets. Mama and Grandma and my sisters didn't want me to be part of their pageant plans. The way they looked at me and Karen and Dana hit me in the gut. They couldn't picture anyone different from them as a pageant girl. Did I even want to work with Charlene? Or with

Grandma, the liar? Here she was getting after me for keeping a secret, when she'd told us a flat-out lie. No, I didn't want to work with them. I stepped back and shook my head. "I'm staying with Miss Vernie and my friends. She's teaching us exactly what we need to know."

"Right." Charlene rolled her eyes and turned on her heel. She started walking away, the wooden soles of her Dr. Scholl's sandals clomping on the sidewalk. Ruthie chased her, and finally Grandma turned to follow.

Then Mama said in a sad, quiet voice, "If that's what you want, Chip. You come home after your haircut." And she turned and caught up to Grandma and the girls.

My stomach was twisting and turning like I was on a roller coaster. I looked down at my bracelet, wondering if I had lost a charm. Nope. I still had two left. Made sense, 'cause I hadn't learned anything new. I already knew I didn't fit in with my family.

Karen rubbed her hand along my arm as Miss Vernie steered me into the salon, but Dana hung back.

My chest was heaving and I was so busy trying to keep the tears from falling, I wasn't even thinking much about my hair. BeBe herself came over and patted the puff of blonde on her head. She pursed her shiny red lips.

"This is . . . interesting," she said, narrowing her eyes at me. She washed my hair and settled me into a different chair in front of a big mirror. Then she combed it out and started cutting big chunks. Karen bit her lip as she watched.

I pressed my eyes closed. I'd always had long hair. I could feel her working above my shoulders and knew my hair was going to be short. If my Daddy was looking for me, he might not even recognize me now.

BeBe blew my hair dry and quickly set a bunch of curls across my head with the curling iron. She brushed it out and spun me around to face the mirror.

"You look so good!" Karen cried, her hands cupped over her mouth. "Like three years older or something. I'm so jealous."

Dana said nothing. I hoped she wasn't mad about what Grandma had said.

"Thanks, it's very nice," I said. But I knew it wasn't pageant hair. Pageant hair was long and flowy. But it wasn't just about the hair. Someone very different was looking back at me, someone with different hair and new, sad eyes. After all this time and all this hard work, my pageant plans weren't helping me get any closer to my family.

chapter eighteen

I WANTED TO GO BACK TO THE POND MORE THAN anything, but Miss Vernie dropped me off at the end of Grandma's driveway 'cause Mama said to come right home after my haircut. I took my time walking up to the front door. I could hear everyone talking and laughing in the living room. Having fun without me. They didn't miss me at all.

They didn't even want me in there. I didn't belong here. Not in Mount Airy. Not in Grandma's house. Not in my family. I was right the day we moved here: I'd never belong. I'd never get Grandma to like me. And that's why I hadn't seen a sign from Daddy.

Because he wouldn't lie to me and let me believe I belonged there when he knew the truth too.

I walked back to Miss Vernie's even though it was suppertime.

"Brenda? Did you forget something?" She was working on the new garden, where she had moved all those red flowers that first day. Karen and Dana had already gone home.

"How are those flowers doing?"

She brushed her hand along her forehead. "They're having a tough time. This summer has been hard. Too hot and too dry. But they're hanging in there." She looked at me. "Sometimes that's all you can do when things get tough—hang in there."

I looked away. "Are things ever tough for you, Miss Vernie?"

She stared off across the garden for a long time. "When things are tough, I just bury my troubles and my heartaches out here." She laughed in a way that sounded like it hurt. "Sometimes I wonder if all those emotions travel up into the flowers and trees, and make 'em stronger."

Her flowers were bigger and brighter than I'd ever seen. The kind you'd expect in a fairy tale. A shower of tiny white petals fell down behind Miss Vernie, but I couldn't tell where they'd come from.

"Is that what you're doing now? Burying your troubles?" I asked her.

"Maybe so. You can join me if you like."

I sat next to her and she handed me a shovel.

"Is this where you come when you think about Charlie?" I asked softly. "That man in the picture?"

She set down her shovel and took off her gardening gloves. She rubbed her eyes. "That's my nephew. The boy I raised. And I do feel that he's out here with me when I work."

I twisted a piece of grass around my finger. "What did you mean when you said you don't know what happened to him? I saw him in his uniform in that picture. Is he a POW or something?" Daddy had told me about the prisoner-of-war soldiers still left in Vietnam.

Miss Vernie stared off for so long I thought maybe she wasn't going to answer me. But then she tilted her head and gave me a sad little smile. "No, he came back from the war. But it had done something to him. Most folks around here were real nice to the vets. But a few people had awful things to say about some of what happened over there during the war." She sighed and seemed to shrink a bit. "Add that to how he was feeling, it was enough to make him leave.

He left me a note saying he couldn't stay here at home with so many reminders of how his life used to be. And how different it had become."

"He left home? On purpose? Where did he go?"

"I don't know. Sometimes I get postcards from different places. They aren't signed, but I think they're from him." She was folding and unfolding her hands. "I don't know. I just don't know. I read all those newspapers from the cities on those postcards, wondering if I'll see some tidbit that'll help me find him. But I think I'm just going to have to wait for Charlie to come back on his own."

I nodded and tried to hold back the tears I felt in my eyes. "I bet you feel real sad losing him like that."

She nodded. "What about you, Chip? Do you have a special space to leave behind some of your sadness?" She brushed my hair away from my eyes. "Because there's so much of it in your eyes."

I nibbled on my lip, wondering if I dare tell her the truth. I blew out my breath. "My daddy died. We aren't supposed to talk about it. Talking about him just makes everyone sad. Especially Mama. I found this one tree I like to climb. But it's far away down the road, by this little creek. I don't feel quite so sad up there. But I haven't been there in a while. That's the kind of thing I used to do, climbing trees. But not now."

Miss Vernie squeezed my shoulder. "There's nothing wrong with being sad. And there's nothing wrong talking about it. If you don't feel the heartache, you just live with it hurting you. It might be hard, all those words coming out at first, but then they're gone. Not so many crowded up inside you." She looked at me, and it hurt my chest to even let the idea flutter around inside me. "But if you don't think you're ready to talk about it with your family quite yet, why don't you work out here in my garden? See if you don't leave some of that sadness behind here in my dirt when you can't make it to your special heartache tree."

So we worked together, ripping out weeds and crabgrass. We didn't even talk. Seemed like everything we needed to say had been said. And each stab of my shovel into the dirt did seem to loosen something inside me.

Eventually Miss Vernie said, "You best get home. I don't need your grandma more upset with me than she already is."

"Why is she upset with you?"

She patted the back of her head, readjusting the updo that was coming undone. "I expect she's angry because I'm working with you, and she's not."

"You're not friends anymore, are you? Is that because you beat her even though she ended up with the crown?"

Miss Vernie turned to me. "How do you know we're not friends anymore?"

"If you were friends, you'd visit each other. Talk to each other on the phone."

She put a hand on my shoulder. "No, that's not the reason we're not friends. Not because of the beauty pageant."

I waited for Miss Vernie to tell me more, but she was quiet as she walked me down the driveway to the road. "You take care now, Brenda."

"I will. You too, Miss Vernie." I felt sad walking home. Somehow those final words seemed like more than just a good night. They seemed like the end of something.

"Where have you been?" Mama shouted when I walked through Grandma's door. "We were worried sick about you. Every day children across America disappear and never see their families again, you know."

"I came home, but you were all busy, so I went to Miss Vernie's."

"We've discussed it, and you're not going back to her school," Grandma said. "The pageant's two weeks away, and we'll be lucky if you don't make fools out of us up there."

I looked at Mama. "I can't go back to Miss Vernie's?" I felt like I was going to throw up.

"I think it's best you work with Grandma," Mama said. "If you want to still do the pageant."

Quitting seemed like a good idea after all these troubles. But this was my only chance for Mama to see me like her. I had to keep at it. "I do. I want to do the pageant with you guys."

Grandma sighed. "I can't imagine what she's been teaching the three of you girls." She untied her apron and threw it on the counter.

"She's been teaching us the baton. My baton is at her house. So's my dress that I bought. I have to go back."

"I'll fetch them tomorrow," Grandma said, "and give her a piece of my mind too."

"Why aren't you two friends anymore, Grandma?"

Grandma's nostrils flared like a dog ready to bite. She opened her mouth, then closed it, and stalked out of the room.

Mama shook her head and Charlene threw up her hands. "Can we get back to practicing my song?"

I headed up to my room and realized Earl was at Miss Vernie's too. Somehow with all this pageant business, I'd forgotten all about him. I'd forgotten about the turtle I promised Daddy I'd save.

It was as bad as forgetting about Daddy.

chapter nineteen

THE SUN WAS JUST COMING UP WHEN GRANDMA
barged into my room. "Up with you now. We've got a
lot of work to do." And she left.

I patted Deady Freddy's head. "At least you like
me." I think he did, anyway.

When I got downstairs, Grandma had a dress laid
out for me.

"Go put this on so you can practice walking like a
lady." She handed me shiny silver high-heeled shoes. I
slipped them on and my ankles wobbled as I went to
my bedroom to get changed.

The dress smelled like mothballs. It was too big,

and it was itchy against my skin. I looked like a little doll that belonged in Grandma's lit-up cabinets. She made me walk back and forth across the kitchen. Then to the front hall, down the stairs, and back up again until lunch.

I could hear Charlene upstairs. Singing, then starting over. Singing, then starting over. And Mama talking softly to her. I wanted Mama to talk like that to me.

Ruthie followed me and Grandma, copying us.

"Such a tiny thing and so good at walking like a lady!" Grandma cooed. But she said nothing like that to me. To me, she just said things like, "Slow down! Can't you smile? Don't stare straight ahead! Look out at the audience."

Finally, at lunchtime, she told me to change out of the dress. We settled around her table. I wished I were headed for the pond with Karen and Dana. We'd never gotten all the cattails out. The thought made tears coat my eyes. I needed somewhere to put all this sadness, like Miss Vernie said. "Do you think I could work out in your garden later, Grandma?"

"My garden is not important. Getting you in shape for this pageant is. We're going to practice your walking some more, then your baton work."

"Did Miss Vernie drop it off?"

"I'm going to go get it while you change back into your clothes."

I thought about asking for my turtle. But Grandma would never let him back in the house.

Two little circles of red burned on Grandma's cheeks when she returned. She thrust the baton at me, hung up my dress, and handed me a book. "Now, put this on your head while you practice your walking."

And that's what we did for the rest of the day. After dinner we went outside, doused ourselves in mosquito spray and practiced the baton until the sun went down. There were no smiles or kind words from Grandma like I'd gotten from Miss Vernie. Maybe Grandma was just a nut I couldn't crack no matter what I did.

"I HEARD THE CROWNS FOR THIS PAGEANT ARE JUST gorgeous," Grandma told us the next day while we were all sitting on the back porch, taking a break from pageant work.

"We'll see for ourselves when I bring one home!" Charlene said, scrunching up her shoulders.

"I'll have to dust off our old crowns, Cecelia, and set them up in the living room cabinets. We'll have room for a couple more." She winked at Charlene.

"I wouldn't be surprised," Mama said.

"Have you prepared your statement for the judges?" Grandma asked me. "You might do well with that portion."

"The statement? What's that?" I asked.

Grandma dropped her head in her hands. "Didn't Miss Vernie teach you anything?"

"Yes. Lots." I swirled the ice in my soda.

"The judges expect you to say a little something about who you are, why you want to be Junior Miss Dogwood 1977, and why you'd be the right girl for the title. Miss Vernie didn't tell you this?"

"We were still working on things. We didn't get to it yet." I ran my fingers over my charm bracelet. Two charms left. But I didn't even know if the bracelet would still work now that I wasn't allowed to go back to Miss Vernie's school.

We practiced walking again until lunch, and then we did more baton work while Mama was putting final touches on Charlene's dress. "Smile, Brenda! You look like you're in pain!" Grandma barked.

Ruthie lay on her stomach in the grass, watching. "Keep trying, Chip!"

"I am," I panted. I didn't realize how hard it would be to twirl a baton in time to music *and* smile.

Later Grandma sat me down after dinner to work on my statement. "So tell me, Miss Brenda Anderson, why do you want to be Junior Miss Dogwood 1977?"

I shrugged. " 'Cause everyone else in my family joined the pageant."

"No! What kind of answer is that? They'll escort you right off the stage." Grandma closed her eyes and pressed two fingers against them. "Most girls would say, 'Because it's such an honor to be part of this long-standing tradition and celebrate all that's beautiful about North Carolina, like the dogwood tree.'"

"Why do they have the Dogwood Festival in the summer? Don't most trees bloom in spring?"

Grandma shook her head and groaned. "The Dogwood is the state tree of North Carolina. But we don't have festivals in the springtime; the weather's too uncertain."

"It seems silly."

"Well, make sure you don't say that to the judges. Everything is great. You're happy as a peach to be part of the Miss Dogwood Festival. Let's try again. So tell me, Miss Brenda Anderson, why do you want to be Junior Miss Dogwood 1977?"

"Because it's a great honor to be part of this lovely festival for such a wonderful tree. And I do enjoy working out in the garden with lovely trees like the dogwood, even though it blossoms in spring not summer." Although, when I thought about it, I wasn't even sure what a dogwood tree looked like.

"Are you trying to be smart?" Grandma's face looked like someone had drawn her with their pencil pressed hard against the paper.

"No, ma'am. Well, yes, I mean. I want to show them I know about nature and trees. Really know when it blossoms. Really care about it. Smart that way."

She smacked her hand on the table. "Don't mention the tree, don't mention the blossoms. It's not about the tree. It's about how sweet and lovely you are, not the tree. Just say this. 'I am new to North Carolina, but I feel like my heart belongs here, especially in lovely Mount Airy. What more could a girl want? I'm so grateful to live in such a wonderful place that represents the best of the South with the Junior Miss Dogwood title.'"

We went over my speech again and again until I almost forgot I didn't mean a word of it.

I THOUGHT WE WERE DONE WITH THE DUMB QUES-tions, but the next day we had to work on another. "So, Miss Brenda Anderson, why are you the right girl to be named Junior Miss Dogwood?"

I stared at her.

"Well?"

"I'm not the right person."

"Well, they're sure to pick you with that answer."

"I'm not from here. I hate dresses. And like you all said, I'm not pageant material." I couldn't believe I said that. I sounded like the old Chip. But working with Grandma wasn't like working with Miss Vernie. She wasn't being nice like she was to my sisters. She didn't seem happy at all that I was joining Miss Dogwood. The only reason I wanted to do this now was to show Mama I could be one of her girls, too, because Grandma didn't care about me at all.

Grandma pressed her fingers against her eyes again. I wondered if she could push them right back into her head until they were stuck. "Okay. This is what you're going to say. 'It takes a certain type of girl to hold a title. One who is charming and beautiful and kind. One who is unique and lovely like the delicate dogwood blossom. I am all those things and would be honored and humbled to represent the Dogwood Festival as Junior Miss.'"

"I thought I wasn't supposed to mention the dogwood flower."

"Just say what I'm telling you to say, Brenda. And you'll be fine. You won't win, but you won't embarrass us. Just try to be a good sport when you lose."

"Is that what you did when you lost to Miss Vernie?"

Grandma's eyes widened and her nostrils flared.

"I know the truth," I said. "You didn't win. Not really. You lied."

Then she slapped me.

It shook the breath out of me. It surprised me so much, I couldn't even ask her why she did it. I touched my hot cheek.

"You're on your own. I don't even care if you embarrass us. You are really not part of this family. Not mine. You are just like your deplorable father and nothing like your beautiful mama."

Grandma stormed out of the room. I felt glued to the chair. No one had ever slapped me before. Cool tears trickled down my skin, wetting the tips of my fingers. I never guessed she hated me so much. I thought about talking to Daddy, but it was clear now that he hadn't been listening to anything. I was all alone down here in North Carolina.

chapter twenty

I CHANGED BACK INTO MY CLOTHES AND RAN OUT OF the house. I sprinted up the street to Miss Vernie's, stumbling and tripping, until I stood in front of her driveway. The trees swayed, almost like they were motioning me to come in, to walk back to the garden. But I didn't know if Miss Vernie was mad at me after Grandma had stormed over to her house. I probably wasn't welcome anymore. So I turned down the street and kept walking and walking and walking until I found that little creek near the tree I had climbed. My heartbreak tree.

I felt under the rocks, looking for some clay or

muck I could squeeze in my hand, but there was nothing like the stuff in Miss Vernie's pond. I searched around for another cool rock, but I didn't find anything. I spent the afternoon skipping stones, chipping away at the picture of Grandma's mean face etched in my brain. And then I went over to my tree and jumped a few times until I could grab the low branch and pull myself up.

I sat in the crook of the arm and wrapped my arms around the trunk. I guess that's where I belonged. Out in the woods by myself where I'd once been so happy with Daddy and Billy. I thought about the time we spotted a rainbow after a thunderstorm, and the three of us went tromping off, determined to find a leprechaun. Daddy never ever told us we were silly for believing in such a thing. And we ended up finding three eagle feathers, a salamander, and a fossil. I rubbed my finger along the bark of the tree. Well, this is where Chip belonged, out in nature. But I wasn't Chip anymore.

I swung my legs off the branch, ready to climb down and go back to Grandma's. But I slipped and fell to the ground.

Pain pulsed through my left ankle. I screamed and grabbed it. It throbbed and hurt so much I threw up on a mossy log in front of me.

"Help!" I cried. "Help!" I kept screaming, but I knew I was so far back in the woods no one could hear me. I tried to pull myself up and walk, but my ankle felt broken. I dragged myself along the dirt of the forest floor, but I only made it a few feet before I crumpled into a ball.

I was going to be one of those hundreds of children across America who disappeared in the woods every day. I closed my eyes and everything went dark.

"BRENDA? BRENDA!"

I winced at the flashlight shining in my face.

"Mama?" I pulled myself up and groaned, feeling the sharp ache in my ankle.

Mama ran over and pulled me into her arms. "Brenda, what happened? Are you hurt?"

I rooted my nose into her long hair. She smelled minty, like Noxzema. "I fell out of the tree. How did you find me?"

"When you didn't come back home for a few hours, we went to Miss Vernie's looking for you. She thought you might be here by the creek."

"Are you okay, Brenda?" Miss Vernie was there too. Her robe hung down under her cardigan sweater.

"I think I broke my ankle." My stomach was empty

and my head was woozy. I looked at Mama's big startled eyes and started crying again. The pageant. How could I be one of Mama's girls with a broken ankle? "I can't be in the pageant like this."

Mama's lip wobbled. "Don't you worry about that now. Let's just get you to the hospital," Mama said. "I told you," she said through her tears. "I told you not to climb those trees. That you'd fall out like all those kids across America who break their legs every day. I was right. No more trees, Brenda."

"Okay." I nodded and sniffed while Mama stood there fretting.

"Shush, now. Everything will be fine." Miss Vernie rubbed Mama's back, and Mama sobbed into her shoulder, nodding. Then, with one arm around Miss Vernie and one around Mama, they helped me out of the woods to Miss Vernie's car. She drove us to the hospital and stayed in the waiting room while they wrapped up my ankle.

"Don't let them cut off my leg, Mama. Not like those hundreds of kids across America every day," I said, my lip trembling.

She kissed my head. "It's just a sprain. You were lucky. I don't think they'll have to take off your leg. You must have an angel watching over you."

I touched the charms on my bracelet and stared

out the hospital window at the stars in the sky. Was she right? Had Daddy been looking out for me?

"You could still compete," said Miss Vernie on the car ride home. "You'll have to modify your baton routine a bit. You've worked too hard to quit, Brenda."

"Thanks, Miss Vernie, but it's more important that Chip heals right now," Mama said.

"No, Mama. I need to do this," I said.

"Why? Why is this so important?" Mama asked.

I couldn't get the right words to come out. "It just is, Mama. You'll see."

Miss Vernie looked back at me in her rearview mirror. "You can come back to school and work with us again any time you like, Chip."

"That's awful kind of you, Miss Vernie, but I want to keep an eye on Brenda," Mama said. Then she turned to me. "If you really want to, I'll help you finish preparing for the pageant."

"But, Mama, you don't have time for me."

"Hush now," she said in a strangled whisper. "Of course I do."

chapter twenty-one

Over the next few days, Mama helped me practice walking with the crutch and spinning the baton while standing in one place. Grandma would walk right by like she didn't even see us. She hadn't talked to me since the day I'd called her a liar, unless it was to ask me to pass the butter or turn off the light in the family room.

I showed Mama my baton routine and she set her arms on my shoulders. "I'm proud of you just for trying," she said.

I grinned.

"You keep at this, now. I've gotta work with

Charlene for a while. She's getting all antsy." She rolled her eyes and walked inside.

For the next week, Mama and I practiced together until I felt like maybe I could make it across the stage and do my routine. I was just happy to be near Mama and feel the soft skin on her hands holding my arms or my shoulders. Just wait until she saw me on that stage.

THE MORNING BEFORE THE MISS DOGWOOD FESTIVAL, I limped downstairs ready for a big day of practicing. But everyone was real quiet at the kitchen table. Grandma had the TV rolled into the kitchen and Mama, Charlene, and Ruthie were all huddled around, watching it.

"What happened?" I asked.

Mama dropped her arms on the table and started sobbing into them, harder than I'd ever seen. Harder even than the night I thought she was a hurt bird. "He's gone." Mama sobbed. "He's gone."

Charlene shook her head like I had caused whatever problem was making Mama so sad. She rubbed Mama's back.

"What?" I limped over to the table.

"Elvis died, Brenda. Yesterday. We just saw it on the news this morning." Charlene kept rubbing

Mama's back. "He was Mama's favorite singer. 'Love Me Tender' was her wedding dance song," she whispered. "You know he was real special to her. She has all his cassettes."

Mama's chest was heaving. She tried to tuck herself into a little ball.

"Mama's crying like that because Elvis died?"

Charlene rolled her eyes and shook her head. Grandma clucked her tongue. Ruthie started crying too.

I skipped breakfast and went outside. I picked out a favorite cloud, one that looked like a ship. One that I thought Daddy would pick to sit on, one that I would climb up to, if I could. "Is she really crying for you, Daddy?" I said to the sky.

Mama stayed in her room all day and I didn't get to practice at all. The next morning, she put on sunglasses first thing. I wondered if she would wear them to the Miss Dogwood Pageant.

After breakfast I dragged myself back upstairs to put on my dress. That would make everyone think twice about me not being good enough for the pageant. They had never seen me in a dress like that and were sure to change their minds.

Oh, Brenda! they'd say. *You are a vision. How*

beautiful! All the kinds of things Charlene always heard. I even put on one shiny white shoe and one leg of my nylons on my good foot. I cut off the side I couldn't wear. We cut the strap off the other shoe so I could fit in my swollen foot. Then I walked down the stairs into the living room. My heart thumped and thumped while I stared at my feet, waiting for the courage to lift my head.

When I did, Mama, Grandma, and Ruthie were watching Charlene. I cleared my throat. They all looked up at me. My lips curled into a smile just waiting for their praise.

"You're interrupting my final fitting," Charlene whined.

Grandma frowned. "Brenda, take that dress off before you get it a mass of wrinkles. You put it on after we get to the pageant hall at the school. Now get changed and get back down here so we can do your hair and makeup."

Mama looked at me. "Do as your grandmother says, Brenda," she said quietly.

No one said a thing about my soft blue dress and my shoes. No one noticed. No one could see Brand-New Brenda standing there. My lip wobbled and I caught my breath before I started crying. Maybe it'd be different when I was onstage. I decided not to say another word until the pageant. I changed out of my dress and went downstairs, waiting for my turn to get made up. I went over my lines to my answers again and again.

Charlene looked like a painting. Her hair floated past her shoulders, and her hair was shiny, as if it had been kissed by the sun. She looked like a beauty queen. I expected all the dolls in the cabinets to start clapping for her.

Ruthie's long curls bounced along her back and she was so pleased with her shiny pink lip gloss that she turned around and around, holding a tiny mirror and smiling at herself. She giggled, and her dimples were little pockets of happiness in her cheeks.

I looked like a head that someone had lopped off a mannequin's body with big startled eyes and hair like a wig plopped on its head. Like I had come to life and couldn't believe I was made of Styrofoam.

Mama looked at me after she finished my makeup and nodded. No one said I looked nice.

WE HAD TO BE AT THE FESTIVAL GROUNDS BY ELEVEN. They were holding the pageant right at the high school, in the gymnasium. The competition started at one. My tummy was already rumbling for lunch when we got there, and the sweet scent of fried dough and cotton candy out in the parking lot made it worse. "Can we get something to eat?"

"No. You don't eat before a pageant," Grandma said. "You want your stomach nice and flat. Besides, it would ruin your lipstick." She didn't even look at me.

We carried our clothes into the girls' locker room. I had my dress and shoes and my baton outfit. Mama had sewn a star made out of sequins onto my red bathing suit. She couldn't make anything fancier for my baton routine in time for the pageant, but I really liked it. It looked kind of dumb with my foot wrapped up, though. I didn't have to use a crutch anymore, but I still hobbled around a bit.

Charlene had two dresses, one for the competition and one for her talent. "I've got a surprise for Mama," she whispered to me.

Mama still had on her glasses and hadn't smiled or said anything in a voice above a whisper since we'd learned the news about Elvis.

Ruthie only had to go onstage once, so she just wore her bright pink dress with white ruffles rolling underneath. She sat on a bench in the locker room with her hands folded on her lap as she waited for us.

"No jewelry, Brenda. Take off that ugly bracelet,"

Grandma said. She held out her hand, waiting for it.

I blinked at her. I couldn't take off my bracelet. Miss Vernie had one rule about being in her school— you always had to wear the bracelet.

"Go on, take it off."

My fingers trembled as I pried open the clasp. The metal slid off my wrist and pooled in my other hand. But I wouldn't give it to her. I set it in the locker with my other things. My breath hitched. This meant I wasn't in Miss Vernie's school anymore.

Grandma shook her head at me. "You really should be in a gown, too, Brenda. It would have covered up that ugly bandage."

I checked out my foot. It did look ugly. "Miss Vernie said the Junior Miss girls should wear party dresses, not gowns."

And that's when Miss Vernie walked by with Karen and Dana.

"There are certain rules to follow in a pageant, certain traditions," Grandma said loudly. "Certain things that should be worn by certain people. A pageant isn't just for anybody," she said, looking at Dana. She slammed the door closed on the locker where she'd put the clothes we'd worn from home. It didn't have a lock, and I hoped nobody would go poking around in there and steal my bracelet.

Miss Vernie kept walking, but Karen turned around and held up her bracelet. "We both lost another charm!" she whispered.

I waited for them to walk past before telling Grandma, "I have to go to the bathroom."

She sighed. "Another reason not to eat or drink anything before the pageant. Hurry up about it."

I shuffled from our section of the locker room, looking for my friends. They were already changed, and Miss Vernie was putting a sparkly necklace on Karen.

"Brenda! Good luck to you. You look just lovely," Miss Vernie said. She opened a locker. "I brought your turtle for you." She paused. "I wasn't sure when I'd see you again, and I didn't think I'd be welcome if I dropped by your grandmother's house. Of course, I can take him home and let him go if you'd like. You can decide after the pageant. He'll be right here waiting for you."

I peered in the bowl. Earl looked more gray than green and didn't open his eyes until I poked him. "Thanks," I said, swallowing a giant gulp of sadness. "So, what lesson did you guys learn when you lost your charms?"

Dana was adjusting her shoes and didn't look up.

"I lost my heart charm," Karen said. "I had a long

talk with my mom about how my stepdad upsets me so much, and she told me he just wants the best for me. That he wasn't really picking on me so much as trying to motivate me to lose weight, to get off the couch and do something. So I guess you could say we had a real heart-to-heart talk. They're both coming today." She smiled so wide, her cheeks looked like they could burst.

"That's great." I fingered my wrist and remembered Grandma made me take off the bracelet. "What about Dana?"

I hoped she would stand up and answer, but she was holding a picture, looking at it. Karen kept talking. "Dana lost her flower charm. She figures it was when she did an interview with the newspaper about being the only black girl in the Miss Dogwood pageant. Guess she felt like she blossomed. There are going to be newspaper reporters here and everything. Maybe even a TV camera! Did you know Jack Taylor, that news anchor, is the MC for the pageant?"

"Wow." A new reason to be nervous. "Well, good luck, you guys."

"You too, Brenda." Miss Vernie looked at me with a smile that seemed more sad than happy.

I held up my wrist. "Grandma made me take my bracelet off for the pageant." My voice dropped to a whisper. "That means I'm not in your school anymore."

She cupped my cheek in her hand. "Don't you worry. You're still in my school if you want to be. I have a feeling there will be a lot to learn right here today."

I didn't think so. I didn't think anything magical or important was going to happen, but I sniffed and nodded and went back to join my family.

chapter twenty-two

THE GYMNASIUM WAS FILLED WITH FOLDING CHAIRS AND a stage that stretched out like the letter *T*. A big curtain hung from the ceiling along the back of the stage, hiding all the contestants lined up on the floor. A set of stairs led to a space on the stage behind the curtain. That's where contestants would wait their turn. I walked along the floor beyond the end of the curtain and peeked out at all those people fanning themselves with programs, their conversations buzzing in the air.

"All the girls go on first in their formal wear," Grandma said. "First the Miss division, then Junior Miss, and so on."

"There are only fifteen girls competing against me," Charlene said, beaming. "I have a real shot."

"Brenda, there are twenty girls in your division, but only eight up against Ruthie. I just know one of you will be walking away with a crown today," Grandma said, looking back and forth between Charlene and Ruthie.

Mama and Grandma sat in the audience with Ruthie. Mama would bring her backstage when it was her turn. Charlene stood off on her own, like the other contestants might scuff up her beauty. I looked more closely and saw she was singing to herself. Probably practicing. But she looked more nervous than I'd ever seen her.

I was glad the talent competition was last. I was antsy about getting my words to the questions to come out right, never mind remembering all the baton moves and balancing on one foot. Climbing a tree was so much easier than this.

I snuck off and sat in a bleacher just beyond the edge of the backstage area so I could see the audience and the end of the runway. There were some very pretty girls in the Miss division. I could tell; they were the ones Charlene was frowning at.

She watched them line up. They all seemed to

know each other, and most of them were glancing at Charlene too. Charlene took her place in line. She was going on sixth, wearing that pale yellow gown that did glow next to her tan skin. Just like Mama said it would.

Charlene looked over at me, and I whispered good luck. She must have been able to read my lips 'cause she smiled. Then she climbed up the stairs to the stage and waited behind the curtain for her turn. I really hoped she would win. She wanted that crown more than a bear wanted honey.

When her turn came, Charlene walked out onstage wearing her big smile and walking her slow, sure walk. I noticed the clapping for her was louder than it had been for the other girls. The contestants who were still lined up backstage whispered behind their hands as they peeked beyond the curtain. Dana was a few places behind Charlene. She was still staring at the picture in her hand, and finally she slipped it down the front of her dress.

Charlene finished her stage walk and came up next to the host for her interview.

"It's time to learn more about our next Miss Dogwood 1977 candidate, Miss Charlene Anderson. Why did you join the pageant, Miss Anderson?" Jack

Taylor smiled as he waited for her answer.

"Thank you, Mr. Taylor. We watch you all the time on the TV."

He blushed. "Why, thanks, darlin'."

Charlene shrugged and showed the crowd her southern belle smile. "I just moved to North Carolina, but I have always been a Southern belle at heart. My mama was runner-up for Miss North Carolina 1963," she said, nodding. "There she is." She pointed to Mama. "The one who looks like Rita Hayworth."

Mama's head snapped up and everyone looked at her.

"She is lovely. I can see where you get your beauty, Miss Anderson," Jack Taylor said.

She nodded. "Thank you, Mr. Taylor. My grandma, right next to her, was Miss North Carolina 1939."

Grandma waved and the audience politely applauded.

Charlene continued. "I think as one of the newest residents of Mount Airy, North Carolina, I can really appreciate what is wonderful about this great state, taking it all in with a fresh eye. I can represent the Miss Dogwood Festival with the energy and enthusiasm I genuinely feel as I discover all that's great about the state of North Carolina. I will be an ambassador who'll make you proud at the many appearances I'll be doing at nursing homes, schools, and grocery store openings. You won't be disappointed when you name me Miss Dogwood 1977."

"You're certainly confident, too, Miss Anderson. Always a good thing. Thank you very much." And he watched her wave to the crowd as she walked off-stage while the judges sat at their table, smiling and scribbling on their notepads.

I could see Grandma holding her hands in the air, clapping. Would she do that for me?

A pretty girl with long black hair named Michelle Dawson went up next, promising to make the Dog-wood Festival a household name in North Carolina. Charlene narrowed her eyes and had her hands on her hips the whole time Michelle was onstage.

Dana was next in line. I wanted to go up to her and wish her good luck. But I just sent her good wish thoughts instead.

The audience hum turned into a buzz as she walked out. A TV camera light turned on. People leaned next to each other and whispered, but Dana just kept her head high, a small, amused smile on her face. She didn't wave and she didn't race across the stage like some of the others had.

Jack Taylor used his important TV voice. "Miss

Dana Jameson, I don't have to point out that you are the only black contestant in a typically white pageant. Why are you the right contestant to represent the Miss Dogwood Festival?"

She looked at him and then stared out at the audience before answering. "Dogwood blossoms come in different colors. Pink and white. Even some yellow. But they're all lovely. I think I am a good representation of the new diversity this nation needs to recognize. Some people think beauty is only a white thing. That I don't belong in this pageant."

I looked at Grandma. She was staring at her hands in her lap.

"Choose me as Miss Dogwood 1977, and North Carolina is saying we recognize beauty no matter what the color of your skin. Or the flower of the beautiful dogwood," Dana finished.

There was polite applause smattered with some loud claps and cheers. I saw one big black man in the back stand up, smiling and clapping.

"Thank you, Miss Jameson," Jack said.

Dana nodded and stood still before the audience, looking them over instead of the other way around. Then she walked off the stage. Dana moved past all of us as she came backstage, and she went right to the locker room. I wanted to follow her, but I was up second in the Junior Miss division and I didn't want to miss my spot. I had no idea she'd shine on stage like that. I hoped I would too.

I practiced my speech while the rest of the girls in Charlene's division went onstage. "My heart belongs here.... My heart belongs here," I mumbled to myself, trying to remember how the rest of my answer was supposed to go.

"Good luck," Karen said to me.

I jumped, surprised to see her standing beside me. "Thanks." I noticed she was still wearing her charm bracelet.

"Wow, your sister is so pretty."

I shrugged. "Dana was something, huh?"

Karen smiled. "She sure was." Karen walked away, looking less like a pastry than when she first tried on the dress. Her posture was different. She didn't slouch, and she didn't hold her hands in front of her tummy. It wasn't her main feature anymore.

I rubbed my own stomach, hoping to calm the bubbles filling up the empty space. I wondered what Daddy would've thought of this. I wondered if he was watching. I got in line and waited for my turn.

The girl before me was tall and skinny. She looked like she could have been in Charlene's division. She smiled at me. "Good luck," she said, in that sweet, southern-pie, sugary way that left you wondering if she really meant it.

A lady with a clipboard waved me right onstage behind the curtain. "You're next!"

I looked back at Karen, two people behind me. She crossed her fingers.

"Next, let's welcome Junior Miss contestant Brenda Anderson, new to Mount Airy, just like her big sister, Charlene, who we met in our Miss division," Jack Taylor said. "Brenda is sporting a sprained ankle."

I walked slowly across the stage, smiling but not looking at the judges or at anyone in the audience, especially not at Mama or Grandma. Each step I took limping on my foot felt like it took a whole minute. Sweat tickled my forehead. The gymnasium was perfectly silent as everyone fanned themselves with their programs and watched my pathetic journey. Laughter and music from the festival outside floated in through the open gymnasium doors.

"Hi, Chip!" I heard Ruthie call. Everyone turned to look. Mama pressed her hand over Ruthie's mouth and smiled. Ruthie was still waving.

This finally made me smile. I waved back and saw Grandma frown.

I turned away from her and walked over to Jack

and blew out a breath; I was going to have to answer his questions now.

"Miss Anderson, why are you the right person to be named Junior Miss Dogwood?"

I took a deep breath and waited for the words to find my mouth. I waited long enough that I could hear whispering start. Then I closed my eyes and remembered the words Grandma made me practice. "I am new to North Carolina, but I feel like my heart belongs here. Especially in lovely Mount Airy. What more could a girl want than to live in such a wonderful place and to represent the best of the South, the Junior Miss Dogwood title?"

"Very nice. Thank you, Miss Anderson. And very, very brave of you to come out with that injured ankle. How'd that happen, anyway?" He scrunched his eyebrows together, all serious.

I looked down at the floor. "I fell out of a tree."

"So you're a tomboy, eh?" He chuckled, and looked out at the audience with a big shrug.

"Well, I used to be. But now I'm . . . different."

"Very well. Ladies and gentlemen, let's have a big round of applause for Brenda Anderson."

I scurried backstage, dragging my foot. I didn't wave or look at anyone.

Karen gave me a thumbs-up sign.

I stayed to watch her go on. She stumbled at first, but she smiled and kept walking. I saw her mom and stepdad in the front row. Her stepdad was taking pictures. I saw a glint of gold bounce off the stage.

When she came back, Karen was glowing. She held up her bracelet. "I lost my last charm—the flower. I have to go show Miss Vernie."

Could Miss Vernie be right? Maybe I would learn something important during the competition too.

chapter twenty-three

I RAN BACK TO THE LOCKER ROOM AND CHANGED into my sparkly bathing suit for the talent competition. I was excited to wear the special outfit Mama had made, but when I saw the other girls in their magnificent costumes, silky material and glitter up and down dresses and body suits, I felt silly in my simple homemade costume. But Mama had done her best.

Luckily, Grandma had insisted we bring long robes to cover ourselves up in case we wanted to go into the audience and watch the competition. I put mine on so I could watch Ruthie.

"Look at this!" said Jack Taylor. "We have another Anderson sister in the competition. This time it's Ruthie Anderson in the first-ever Little Miss division."

Ruthie stopped and waved at the audience. She covered her giggle with her gloved hand. I chuckled, watching her.

Jack knelt down beside her. "Why do you want to be the first ever Little Miss Dogwood?"

She locked her hands behind her back. "Grandma said I should join because I'm so precious."

The audience laughed and I saw Grandma looking around, forcing her frown into a smile.

Ruthie grabbed the mike from him, remembering her line. "And because North Carolina is a beautiful place and the dogwood is a beautiful tree and I want to tell everyone how much I love them!" Sure enough, she sounded like she'd been living in North Carolina all her life. Just like Charlene. And then she turned on that big old smile.

"Well put," said Jack. "Can I have my mic back now, darlin'?" He held out his hand and grinned at the audience.

"Sure. Let me show you my talent. My sister Chip, I mean—*Brenda*—taught me this." With that, Ruthie put her nose to the stage, stuck her rump in the air and shook it back and forth. Then she rolled over in a perfect somersault. She stood up and threw her hands in the air while the audience howled.

I wondered what color Grandma's face was: white or red. I couldn't tell. Her hands were covering it.

"Thank you, Ruthie Anderson. And that was a little bonus, ladies and gentlemen, because the Little Miss contestants aren't even required to have a talent portion." Jack raised his eyebrows.

Ruthie skipped off the stage, blowing kisses and waving.

I ran backstage where Mama was waiting for Ruthie. Finally, Mama was smiling.

Charlene was not. "They are going to take points away from my score because I'm related to you two. I just know it! Ruthie acted just like Chip out there." Her fists were planted on her hips and she was wearing her talent gown, a white dress with silver sparkles. She looked beautiful but mean.

She looked like Grandma.

Ruthie started crying and Charlene stomped off.

Mama smoothed Ruthie's hair and kissed her. "I thought you were wonderful. You were just being you, Ruthie. And we love who you are."

Mama smiled at me and led Ruthie to sit back down in the audience. Heads turned to watch Ruthie go by. I could just imagine Daddy laughing, too, saying, "Would you look at that little one? Would you look at my girl?"

What would he say about me?

I sat down next to Mama and Ruthie to watch Charlene's talent segment. I had to admit, she sure could sing.

When Jack Taylor introduced her, his big smile returned. "Let's welcome back Miss Charlene Anderson, sister of the delightful Ruthie and Brenda!"

Charlene's grin slipped a bit, but she forced it up.

"What will you be performing today?"

"I will be singing, Mr. Taylor, but I have a last-minute change in my selection." She looked down at the floor, all sad.

"Oh?" He sounded confused.

"Yes. In light of yesterday's tragic death of the King himself, Mr. Elvis Presley, I would like to honor his memory with a song. A song that is precious to the hearts of so many. Especially my mama."

The piano started playing, and Charlene began singing "Love Me Tender." The audience murmured and Mama's hand hovered over her mouth.

Charlene's voice wobbled a bit when she saw Mama press both her hands against her face. But she closed her eyes and kept on singing, swaying to the song, clenching her hands in front of the microphone.

"Thank you. Thank you very much," Jack said quietly when she finished. Charlene nodded like she had performed some important duty, and went backstage. She got a real nice round of applause. I couldn't tell if it was out of respect for Elvis or Charlene.

I shifted in my seat, uncomfortable about my own talent, wondering if I could do it. And not just because of my ankle. I was okay at the baton, but it wasn't something I loved. I wished I had something like that. Something I loved so much it could squeeze any bad feeling out of my heart.

People sat up, interested, when it was Dana's turn. The audience went silent as she walked out in a traditional African dress of vibrant oranges, yellows, and browns. Even I knew it was not a pageant gown.

"Miss Jameson is back. And I'm told we have another singer," Jack said.

"Yes, and this song is in honor of the real king. Dr. Martin Luther King, Junior, whose light has not been dimmed even though he is no longer with us."

I waited for the piano or some sort of music to start, but all I heard was Dana's sweet voice, quiet at first then louder as she sang the words to "This Little Light of Mine."

Her voice was strong and lovely and hung on all the right words, like not hiding her light under a bushel, and how she was going to let it shine all over the world. She held the last note so long I wasn't sure when she'd stopped. Then the clapping started, a loud thunderous clapping. It was the tall black man in the back again. Quite a few people stood up, until most everyone joined the standing ovation.

I stood up too, and I clapped my hands till they stung. Dana was never going to be my best friend, but we were closer than the first time we'd met. I was so proud of her for going out there and being herself, no matter who was looking down their noses at her. No matter if it cost Dana the crown. Watching her, the same good feeling bubbled up inside me like the day we first slathered mud over our faces in the pond. She was being herself and it was beautiful. Just like Miss Vernie had always told us. Just like Daddy had once told me too.

The crowd went on clapping for so long, they made the next girl in line wait to go out onstage for her talent. Out of the corner of my eye I saw Charlene stomp off to the locker room.

And I followed. I had some changes to make.

By the time I'd returned, my robe tied tight around me, holding what I needed, it was almost my turn. I saw Miss Vernie in the corner. She smiled at me like she knew. Like she knew what I was going to do.

I took off my robe and limped up the stairs behind the curtain. The lady with the clipboard squinted at me. "Why aren't you dressed for the talent competition?" she asked.

"I am."

Her eyes swept over me and landed on the birthmark on my cheek, no longer covered up by makeup. "All right then. Go ahead."

I went out onstage in my jean shorts and T-shirt and charm bracelet, holding Earl in his plastic bowl.

"Our second Anderson sister, Brenda, is back," he said with a curious note in his voice. "I was told you had a baton act."

"I have a different talent to tell you about. It's not something I can really show you. It's not really pageant material. Neither am I, really. My name is Brenda, but people call me Chip. I can climb trees, but sometimes I fall out of them. I can take care of flowers. Even turtles. This is my pet turtle, Earl. I found him, and I've been taking care of him because he was all alone."

I showed Jack my bowl, and he made an exaggerated face like he was real interested.

"Anyway, my other talent is being myself. My daddy always told me he loved me just the way I was. I guess I forgot that. And I know Daddy's watching from heaven today. And I know he'd be disappointed in me, out here pretending I like dresses and twirling the baton. So I guess those are my talents, Mr. Taylor. Loving nature and being myself."

Everyone was quiet. Even Mr. Taylor. "Those are very important talents. We certainly want our Miss Dogwood to be a nature lover. And to be true to herself. Thank you, Brenda."

"It's Chip," I said. "My name's Chip." I stopped and looked out at the audience, a big smile on my face. Mama smiled back at me and set her hand over her heart. When I heard a tiny clink on the stage, I figured my ballet slippers had fallen off, even though I wasn't really, totally, standing on both feet. I was mostly standing on my right foot because my other foot was all wrapped up.

Miss Vernie was waiting for me backstage with a big hug.

But then Charlene burst between us. "You just ruined my chances of winning! I swear you are not my sister." She pointed her finger at my wrist. "And take that dumb bracelet off. I bought one just like it at Woolworth's. All the stupid charms kept falling off." She stalked away.

I looked at Miss Vernie, my stomach swirling. "Is that where you get the bracelets?" I figured it was some exotic, faraway place. Not Woolworth's on Main Street where anybody could get one.

She nodded and put her soft hand on my cheek. "It is, Brenda. But did you ever think it might not be the bracelet that's magic, but the person wearing it?"

I pulled back from her. My heart was in my throat. She made us think the bracelets were special. Important. Wasn't this just like Grandma tricking us about winning the crown? I crossed my arms and I could feel my chest heaving. I wouldn't look at her.

"Do you think you learned anything?" Miss Vernie asked. "*I* think you did."

I blinked back fresh tears. "I did learn something each time a charm fell off, but how did that happen if the bracelet isn't magic?"

She stepped toward me, put her hands on my shoulders, and peered right into my eyes. "People who find my school are always searching for something. They're looking for the lessons to help them find it. Losing charms just makes sure they're paying attention, thinking about what they might be learning along the way. Because there's always a lesson if you're paying attention. And whether you think that's magical is up to you."

Miss Vernie's warm blue eyes were fixed on me, and I thought of how sad and lonely I was the first day I went to her school. I didn't feel like that now. I looked at my bracelet, and I remembered the charms I'd lost and the lessons I'd learned.

My heart stopped spinning and I felt like it was filling up with something warm and soft and bright. I smiled. "I think it *is* magic, Miss Vernie. And I bet Charlene didn't learn a thing."

"Probably not," she said, shaking her head. "It doesn't work for just anyone, you know."

I nodded. Turns out, most of the things I learned at Miss Vernie's School of Charm didn't have much to do with the pageant, and that was fine. But nothing had taught me how to fit in with my family, and nothing had helped settle my heart back into place. Maybe I was just going to have to get used to that feeling.

chapter twenty-four

I CHANGED BACK INTO MY GOWN LIKE ALL THE OTHER girls had and then I left my turtle with Miss Vernie. After a little while all the contestants were called back onstage for the judges' decision. We lined up by division, except for Ruthie, who ran over to me and held my hand.

"We're going to start with our Miss Dogwood division," Jack Taylor said. "We had fifteen wonderful contestants this year. The judges truly had a difficult time picking a winner. So we will start with our runners-up. In third place, Miss Charlene Anderson, one of our newest North Carolina residents."

Charlene froze and then smiled. Her eyes were big and blank. She walked up to Jack Taylor, who placed a small crown on her head. She stood off to the side, still smiling in that weird way; it was exactly how Mama smiled in that runner-up picture of hers.

"Our second-place finisher was very close in points to our first-place winner. We want to say congratulations to Miss Dana Jameson!"

All the hardness fell off Dana's face. She walked, in what felt like slow motion, to the front of the stage. Jack set the crown on her head, placing it high on her Afro. Loud pockets of cheers came from the crowd. Dana stepped next to Charlene, who gave her another fake smile.

"And finally, Miss Dogwood 1977. Miss Michelle Dawson!" She was the tall black-haired girl who Charlene had frowned at the entire time.

Michelle walked out like she'd been expecting the crown all along. Her hands cupped her mouth, and then she kissed Jack Taylor on the cheek. He slapped his hand over the spot and pretended to stumble back in awe. The audience laughed and cheered.

Once the winners had given each other fake hugs, smoothed their sashes, and settled down, Jack addressed the crowd. "Now for the Junior Miss division."

Please be Karen, I thought. *Please be Karen.* I knew

I didn't have a chance anymore.

But he didn't call Karen's name. It was another one of the girls. My heart sank a little. To me, Karen would always be number one, but I doubted the judges would've placed her higher than third.

"And in second place, a contestant whose beauty showed inside and out, Miss Brenda Anderson! I mean, Chip!" Jack Taylor corrected.

I blinked and shook my head, like maybe I was hearing things wrong. But Jack Taylor was staring at me, waiting. I was stuck to the stage floor until Karen pushed me. I must've floated up there because I don't remember walking. Jack set the crown on my head. It slipped off and we both bent to pick it up. We bonked heads and everyone laughed. But I didn't care. I wasn't nervous Brenda Anderson trying to be a beauty queen. I was just Chip, being herself.

I clapped loudly for the pretty girl who had gone on before me and who'd won the title. She really was beautiful, and I bet she'd win the Miss division the next year.

"And finally it's time for the very first Little Miss Dogwood." He opened the envelope and shook his head. "Those Anderson girls. Ruthie Anderson is our Little Miss Dogwood."

Ruthie did another somersault, landing at Jack's

feet. She jumped up, reaching for the crown. And when he put it on her head, she ran over to me. A hurt look flashed in Charlene's eyes.

"And there you have it! A very memorable, very special Miss Dogwood pageant," Jack said.

We filed off the stage and the newspaper photographers and TV station reporters were lined up, waiting to interview the winners. We all posed for a newspaper picture. The big flashbulb blinded me as I stood there with my little crown.

When the photographer was done, I looked for Dana to congratulate her. But she rushed past me and a picture fluttered from her hand. I picked it up and examined the old black-and-white photo of a very pretty woman with blond hair sitting on a picnic blanket, smiling.

I chased after Dana, carrying the picture, but I stopped when I saw her talking to the tall black man who had clapped so loudly for her. He talked to her for a few moments and then hugged her. And I saw the last charm fall from her bracelet.

I walked over with her picture. "You dropped this. And your charm." I pointed to the ground.

She looked at her bracelet and smiled. "Dad, this is my friend Brenda from Miss Vernie's."

"Chip," I said, holding out my hand.

He shook my hand. "It's very nice to meet you. Hope that ankle of yours gets better soon. That charm school sure did teach you two a lot. And you both got a crown." He grinned at us again. "I'll be right back, baby, I'm gonna go pull the car up." We watched him walk away.

"Your dad sure claps loud. I could hear him over everyone."

Dana grinned. "He was real proud of me even though I didn't win."

"You came in second. That was great."

She nudged me with her elbow. "So did you. You really surprised me, walking out there with your turtle, girl."

"When I saw you up there being yourself, I knew I had to do the same thing. That's what Miss Vernie always said. Why wasn't I listening?"

"Guess sometimes it takes a while to know what's right." Then Dana smiled at me. For the first time, she really smiled at me.

I handed her the picture. "Who is this?"

She took it, letting out a big sigh. "That's my mama. But you'd never know it. She looks more like you than me."

I shrugged. "I don't look like my mama either. Not at all."

"That's why I joined the pageant." Dana rubbed her thumb over the picture. "I wanted to compete with white girls like my mama 'cause no one thinks someone like me could. I wanted to show her—I wanted to show everyone."

"Well, I was wrong, Dana. Everyone was. This was the perfect pageant for you."

She looked back at the picture. "I used to think that's why she left—'cause she couldn't see herself in me. But my dad and I had a long talk the other day when I was showing him my dresses for the pageant. We'd never really talked about why Mama left. Daddy just always told me she had to leave. Turns out, she thought life would be easier for me and dad without her. Not everyone was real happy about them getting married. She didn't leave because of me. I suppose that's why I lost my heart charm. Being up there onstage, holding my head high . . . well, the pain doesn't hurt quite as much now."

"I bet your mama would be proud of you, Dana. Just like I bet my daddy would be proud of me. I'm glad we were in Miss Vernie's school together."

She wrapped her arm around my shoulder. "Me too."

I went back to join my family. Mama and Grandma and my sisters were waiting for me in a tight little knot as they fussed over crowns and sashes. I fingered my bracelet. The heart charm was still there. Sure seemed like I should've lost it. What else could I have to learn?

"Well, that was an unusual pageant," Grandma said, tucking her purse under her arm. "Next year we won't be taking part in the Miss Dogwood Pageant. We'll head straight for the top." She pointed her finger up to the ceiling. "Junior Miss North Carolina."

Charlene pulled Ruthie in front of her and set her hand on her head. "What do you think, baby girl?"

Ruthie shrugged. "I liked this pageant. And we all won."

I smiled at Ruthie and saw Miss Vernie coming toward us. "Congratulations, Chip."

Grandma stepped in front of her. "I should report you to the authorities for running a school like that," she said. "It's a sham!"

Miss Vernie's shoulders dropped. And so did her voice. "Nancy, I closed that charm school when my Charlie left." She shrugged. "But people kept showing up. And people kept finding what they needed there. Still do." She put her arm around me.

"I've never noticed a sign," Grandma said.

"Seems like the only people who see it are the ones who need my school." She pulled a charm bracelet from her pocket and handed it to Grandma.

"What's this?"

"Chip can explain how it works. Let's consider it a peace offering."

Grandma turned red and refused the bracelet. But she didn't stare down Miss Vernie like I figured she would. Grandma was looking at the floor. "I wasn't the only one upset after the war," she said. "I wasn't the only one who said those things to Charlie."

Miss Vernie held up her hand. "I buried that heartache not too long ago." She winked at me and smiled. The bracelet lay curled in her palm, and she pressed it into my hand. "I'll leave this with you, Chip. You all enjoy the rest of your day."

Miss Vernie walked away, leaving behind her a sweet, comforting smell.

"Let's go home," Grandma said.

"For cheesecake and china?" Ruthie asked.

Grandma shook her head. "No, we won't be celebrating this pageant. This pageant didn't follow tradition."

I swallowed and bit my lip so I wouldn't cry. I'd been dreaming about that fancy dinner and sitting with everyone talking about the big day. Was this just because of me?

Mama stood up straight and narrowed her eyes.

She pointed a finger at Grandma. "We are coming home with three crowns!" She held up three fingers. "My girls won them, and we are celebrating tonight. We are not skipping this tradition just because you didn't like how things were done. We feast like queens after pageants. That's what the Coopers do—and now the Andersons too." Her voice was strong and a bit too loud. "And when you get home, you're going to let these girls pick out a doll like you promised." She crossed her arms and nodded.

Grandma's faced turned white and she blinked at Mama. Then she nodded too. "Very well. Let's go home and get ready."

I looked at Charlene and we shared a quick smile. Mama was back.

chapter twenty-five

AFTER WE GOT HOME, I WENT OUTSIDE AND SET EARL'S bowl on the patio. I kept my crown on. I was surprised how much I liked the feel of it. Plus, I wanted to remind everyone that I had won it. I'd really won it! I sat down in the grass and stared up at the sky for a while, wondering if Daddy could see it sparkling on my head.

I heard the screen door slam and looked up to see Charlene stalking through the grass toward me. "Don't think that crown makes you pageant material," she said, jutting one hip to the side. "You're not. I was right about that. You got lucky."

The sun shone right behind her, and I squinted up to look at her face, holding the crown on my head with one hand. "I know. And I don't care."

She was quiet for a while, some of the anger seeping off her as she stared into the woods. She plopped next to me on the ground and plucked a blade of grass. "You know, you might not be beauty pageant material, but you sure are strong—like what you did today . . ."

I leaned back. "Me? Strong?"

She picked a tiny daisy and tucked it behind her ear. "Yeah. That's what Daddy always said. That you were strong. A regular chip off the old block. I heard him say that to Mama lots of times."

"A chip off the old block?"

She cocked her head. "Yeah. Like your nickname."

I shook my head. "He called me Chip cause of my chipped teeth."

She raised an eyebrow, looking confused. "No. He was telling Mama you were so strong and brave when you fell out of the tree that you didn't even cry. Not at the dentist, either. That you were a strong little chip off the old block."

"What? No way. I'm not strong like Daddy."

Charlene gave me her favorite *Ican'tbelievehow dumbyouare* look. "He meant a chip off the old block like *Mama*. Strong like her. He said I had Mama's outsides but you had her insides. And he said that's what he loved most about Mama. Her insides." Her voice got high and squeaky by the time she finished. Her eyes were shining and she snapped her head away from me.

My throat tightened and I didn't know what to say. My head was spinning with this news. *Strong like Mama?* I let out the breath I was holding. "Thanks. For telling me that."

I *was* like Mama. We did have something that was the same, even if it was something you couldn't see. It was something that had been there all along.

Charlene picked a dandelion and tossed it aside. "You're lucky. There's nothing about me that's like Daddy." She swallowed and then sniffed. "I should have spent more time with him. Like you did." She hung her head and her hair formed a curtain, covering her face. "You were his favorite. He loved you best."

I shook my head so hard I felt woozy, like I was on a carnival ride. "No, Charlene. He loved us all. All the same. Maybe he just loved me different because we were so much alike, we could do more things together. But he was always talking about you and Mama and Ruthie when we were exploring the woods. Honest. He said he was the luckiest man in the world thanks to us girls. And Mama."

She pressed her lips together and tried to hold back a big sob ready to tumble out. "I miss him so much I can't even find the words to talk about it," she said in a whisper.

I reached over and patted her hand and she grabbed it and held it tight. "Why not try talking to him? I do it all the time."

She looked at me funny. "He doesn't answer, does he?"

I smiled. "Not with words. But I'm hoping that he hears me." I wasn't sure about that yet; I hadn't really seen a sign from Daddy.

She let go of my hand, then curled a strand of her hair around her finger and nodded.

"Holding in the sadness doesn't make it go away," I said. "It's still there inside you."

She sniffed again. "It hurts to talk about it."

"It hurts more not to." I looked down at the ground. Charlene was digging her toes in the grass. A tiny daisy was stuck between her toes. My eyebrows shot up. "You know, Charlene, you're wrong."

"About what?"

"You've got something just like Daddy. Something I don't have at all."

She narrowed her eyes at me. "What?"

I pointed to her foot. "Your second toe is longer than your big toe. Just like Daddy's was. He always said that second toe was trying to overthrow the big toe and that he better keep an eye on it. That's why he walked around barefoot so often."

Charlene stared down at her toes and wiggled them. She started laughing and gave me a playful push. "All these years and I never knew."

"See? I'm a little bit like Mama, and you're a little bit like Daddy after all."

She tucked my hair behind my ears and straightened my crown. "And sometimes you're even like me," Charlene said.

I leaned back from her like she was crazy. "How?"

She lifted her shoulders in a quick shrug. "You can be cool. But only once in a while." She stood up and winked at me and walked back inside, letting the screen door slam behind her.

I smiled so wide, it hurt. I had a little bit of everybody in me. But what about Grandma? I thought about the off-limits room and all the secrets she was hiding. Once upon a time Grandma had been like me. She'd loved animals. She'd been a daddy's girl and a tomboy. But was that little girl gone forever?

I went into the living room where Mama sat on

the couch with Ruthie on her lap while Grandma was putting the new crowns in the display case next to hers. I handed mine to Grandma. "I won't be getting another one of these."

Grandma took the crown and looked at it for a long while. "You could try again, Brenda," Grandma said in a soft voice I hadn't heard before. "Even with all your shenanigans today, you won a crown. I know this pageant was a hard thing for you to do. With a little work, who knows what you could do?" She swallowed. "I could help you. I've been thinking we could do better together next time."

I nodded and tucked my hands in my pockets. I didn't want to be angry at Grandma anymore. And I was done trying to be someone I wasn't. "I'm sorry too. But Grandma, you and Charlene were right. I'm not a pageant girl. I like the woods and animals and nature." I shrugged. "That's who I am. You used to like those things too, right?"

She opened and closed her mouth and looked at the floor. "It's true. I did."

I shrugged again. "If you ever want to go for a walk in the woods, let me know. But I don't want to be in another pageant." I looked at Mama and turned up my hands. "Besides, I heard hundreds of kids across America every day are rushed to the emergency room with horrible headaches from these great big heavy crowns."

Mama laughed and set Ruthie down. She came over and pulled me into a hug. "That's my girl."

My throat tightened hearing those words and I squeezed her back. "I know, Mama."

She released me from our hug when Grandma called us over. "Girls, it's time to pick out your dolls," Grandma said.

Ruthie clapped and Charlene looked excited. "This is so nice of you," Charlene said.

The three of us spent a long time looking over the dolls, deciding which ones we liked best. Ruthie had one in each hand and kept changing her mind. I spotted the one I wanted on the bottom row. A smiling girl with wooden shoes and a handful of tulips. I pointed to it. "Can I have that one, Grandma?"

Grandma bent down and took it out of the case. She smoothed down the dress and studied it. "I got this doll when I turned forty."

"I like it best because of the flowers."

"Me too." She handed it to me. Then she turned to help Charlene and Ruthie.

"Thank you, Grandma."

She hesitated, then quickly wrapped an arm around my shoulder. "You are very welcome." She looked back at me. "Maybe I could move some of those boxes of material out of your room and set up some shelves so you can display your things, Brenda."

"That would be great. Thank you, Grandma."

"It's Chip, Mother," Mama said.

"Yes, that's right," Grandma said.

"Do you all mind if I go outside for a while?" I asked.

"Go right ahead, darlin'," Mama said.

"Be home by eight!" Grandma said. "We'll have our celebration dinner ready."

"Don't worry. I won't be climbing any trees."

"You did well," Miss Vernie said without even looking up to see who was standing by her.

I set down Earl's bowl. "Thanks. But I'm confused. I didn't lose my last charm."

She stood up and took my face in her hands, tipping my head so I was looking at her. "But you gained so much today. That charm will come off. I promise you."

And that's when I noticed the tree behind her. It had the same flowers with the four petals as the one I had fallen out of back home, way back when I'd chipped my teeth; only these petals were a creamy yellow, not white. "That tree is blossoming. I thought trees only blossomed in spring?"

Miss Vernie threw up her hands. "I know. But this here dogwood opened up this morning flush with new blossoms." She picked one and twirled it between her fingers.

A lump caught in my throat. "That's a dogwood?" All this time, I never knew what kind of tree had been in our front yard. Mama always called it "that dang tree" since it made me chip my teeth.

"Yes. Beautiful, isn't it?" Miss Vernie nodded. "I'm so glad to see these flowers again. Maybe the hot dry summer confused it and made it bloom again." She tilted her head, looking at the tree. "Although, as I remember, back in the spring, the flowers were white. They're different now, but still lovely."

I fingered one of the flowers on the tree. "They're nice."

"Especially the second time around."

"Why would it blossom again?"

We stared at it together. "Stress sometimes does that to trees and plants. Kind of like the way hot water brings out the tea. Stress can change things. Sometimes even people."

"But your garden didn't dry up this summer. Not like Grandma's."

"It's a special place back here, Chip. Sometimes

when something happens like that, it's a sign. A tree flowering when it shouldn't—that can be a sign to pay attention or a sign you're not alone."

"A sign?" My heart thundered in my chest. I expected Daddy could hear it all the way from heaven, just like I could feel him now. Tears blurred my vision as I stared at those beautiful flowers covering the tree. Then I thought about the lily pads and the dandelions and all the wonderful things that had happened in Miss Vernie's garden. And I wondered if Daddy had been sending me signs all along from the moment I'd stepped into Miss Vernie's school of charm and I just hadn't seen them. Daddy had been listening, after all.

I blew out a breath that I felt like I'd been holding for months. And a peaceful feeling washed over me. For the first time since we'd moved down here, my heart wasn't hurting. It was back in place.

"There are always signs around us, Chip, if you know what to look for. You make sure you keep looking for them."

"I will." I nodded and looked down at Earl. I figured he had been a sign too. But it was time to say good-bye. I expected to feel a lump in my throat, but I didn't. "Can I put Earl in your pond, Miss Vernie?"

Miss Vernie smoothed the hair along the back of

my head. "It'd be a nice place for him. I think he'd adjust real fine."

We walked down the path together. It seemed to take a lot longer than usual.

I stood in front of the pond and stared at the ripples rolling across the surface from the soft breeze. The sun slipped behind a cloud. I picked up Earl and kissed the back of his shell. I cupped him in my hand, just like I did when I picked him up the very first time. "I think you're going to be okay now. I think you're ready to go," I whispered to him. Then I set him on the shore. He scooted down into the pond, and I watched him swim away until the only thing I could see was the trail of mud he kicked up.

"You lost your heart," Miss Vernie said, pointing to the glint of gold settled in the muck by the shore.

I looked at her and smiled. "No. Just my heart-ache." I handed her the empty bracelet.

"Keep it," she said. "It might be nice to fill it up now, with the things you love. In fact, I have a charm waiting, just for you." She reached into the pocket of her dress and handed me a small flower charm. A dogwood blossom.

I attached it to my bracelet and hugged Miss Vernie like I was saying good-bye for good. I knew she lived just down the road, and that I could see her any time. But I knew someone else would need Miss Vernie's school soon.

"I'm here whenever you need me," Miss Vernie said, walking away.

And somehow that was enough.

I sat on the bank and waited. I knew Karen and Dana would show up eventually. We had a job to finish.

WE PULLED THE LAST BATCH OF CATTAILS OUT JUST before the sun started slipping past the trees. Only this time, I swapped spots with Dana because of my sprain. I stood on shore and hauled them out the best I could, a plastic bag wrapped around my foot.

As I walked home from Miss Vernie's school for the very last time, it finally started to rain after weeks and weeks of that hot, dry weather. When I stepped into Grandma's house, the smell of beef and onions filled my nose. It felt like home.

"I'm going upstairs to change!" I hollered. "I'll be right down."

"Hurry up, Chip! Our feast fit for a queen is almost ready to start!" Ruthie hollered back to me.

I dashed into my room and stripped off my dirty shorts. Something sitting on the bed caught my eye. It was a tiny wooden turtle right on the middle of my quilt. I picked it up and smoothed my finger over the shiny wood. It was almost the same size as Earl. I'd seen this turtle before. It was from the cabinet in Grandma's off-limits room.

I grinned. "How about that, Daddy?"

I set the turtle down next to Deady Freddy and pulled on the cherry-sundae dress Grandma had given me and rushed for the stairs. Then I paused in front of the off-limits room. Knowing no one could see me, I twisted the knob on the door. It turned. The off-limits room wasn't locked.

"You coming, Chip?" Mama called.

I stepped back from the door, smiling. "I sure am."

The next morning, I didn't sneak out of the house like I had for most of the summer. I didn't feel like being alone out in the woods. I wanted to be with my family. I sat down at breakfast with a smile. "Since I'm done with pageants, do you think we could start on a new project, Grandma?"

She looked up like she was surprised I was talking to her. Her mouth parted, but she didn't say anything.

"We've got to do something about your gardens. What do you say we plant a dogwood tree out back so we can all enjoy the blossoms next spring?"

Grandma was silent, but Mama stood up and placed her hands on my cheeks. "I think that would be a wonderful thing for all of us to do together. We could plant it in memory of your daddy. It would be a real nice way to remember someone who enjoyed nature just as much as his little Chip."

Grandma looked up at me. There was a speck of softness opening up in her eyes. "Yes, that would be just fine . . . Chip."

"Look at this," Mama said, handing me the newspaper.

I took it from her and saw the big picture she had pointed to. It was a picture of all the Miss Dogwood winners. Sure, my eyes were closed. But I was in the newspaper! "This is the Coolest Thing Ever!" I cried. "Can I have it?"

"Sure," Mama said. "Grandma bought ten copies in town this morning before you girls got up."

I hurried to my room and pulled a pair of scissors from Grandma's sewing kit. Then I bounced onto the bed and took out my stationery. "Would you just look at this, Deady Freddy! I'm in the newspaper." I knew he would have hooted his approval if he could have.

I cut out the picture and folded it up in an envelope. Then I got out a sheet of paper.

Dear Billy,

I know you'll think this is the Stupidest Thing Ever, but look! I came in second in a beauty pageant down here. Or maybe you'll think it's the Funniest Thing Ever, but really, the way it all worked out was the Coolest Thing Ever. Really.

Things are getting better, and I think I might end up liking it here. But I'll never forget all the fun we had. And I hope you'll keep writing to your new North Carolina friend.

I paused, unsure how to sign it. I wasn't a brand-new Brenda, but I wasn't the old Chip either. I smiled, figuring out what to write.

Your pal,
A brand-new Chip

september 1983

GRANDMA CLICKED OFF THE TV. SHE DIDN'T SAY ANY-
thing for a while. None of us did. "At least she made
the top ten."

"Yeah. But Charlene won't see it that way," I said.

Grandma nodded and stretched. "I best be getting
to bed so I can get up early and make one of my peach
pies. Maybe two. She'll be looking for some conso-
lation when she and your mama get home, and my
peach pie usually does the trick." Grandma headed
up the stairs to her room.

"Good night, Grandma," I said.

"Night, Grandma," Ruthie called. Then she

turned to me. "I thought the winner really was the prettiest. But don't tell Charlene."

"Don't worry. I'm not going to say anything about the Miss America pageant unless she does."

"I, like, can't believe I was ever in a pageant," Ruthie said, twirling a ringlet of hair round her finger.

"You were in a few of them, Ruthie," I said. "And you won them all."

She shrugged, and then retied her curly dark hair into a ponytail. "Yeah, well, gag me with a spoon. That's all I have to say. Want to go exploring in the morning? Look for the Coolest Thing Ever? Who's winning now?"

"Billy. He sent me a picture of the two-headed snake he caught in the woods."

She snapped her fingers. "Dang. We'll have to look real hard."

"Maybe tomorrow afternoon. I've got something to do in the morning."

I headed up to my room and crawled into bed, after patting the owl first, like I always did. "You missed it, Deady Freddy. A black girl won Miss America."

That night I dreamed about Dana and Miss Vernie and a pond full of muck.

I GOT UP EARLY THE NEXT MORNING AND HEADED DOWN the road. In the six years since that summer, I hadn't been back to Miss Vernie's, though I'd chatted with her in town a few times. Grandma and I seemed to add a new garden bed to our backyard every year. Ruthie liked to help us too. And we planted something new every year that we thought Daddy would've liked. We even sold all Grandma's dead animals—except for Deady Freddy—and set up tables with growing lights downstairs in the basement so we could raise our own petunias and marigolds and prize-winning roses.

Oftentimes I'd think, *I have to stop by Miss Vernie's.* But somehow I never made it there. I was sure she was busy with the new students who had found her. But that morning I needed to see her.

I put on my charm bracelet and fingered the dogwood blossom as I walked to her house. I touched the others I'd added along the years: a cattail, a rose, a tree, and a turtle. When I peeked behind Miss Vernie's house, she looked up like I had just been there yesterday. And I wasn't at all surprised to see Dana there too. I'd only seen her and Karen a few times since our summer with Miss Vernie, since we all attended different schools.

"Were you watching last night?" I asked her.

Dana nodded and smiled. "Yeah, wow. A black Miss America." Her hair was cropped and dyed a bright burgundy color. But I would have spotted her anywhere.

"That could have been you," I said. "You should have kept competing after the Miss Dogwood Festival."

Dana picked a flower off one of Miss Vernie's bushes, which were bigger than ever. "Nah, I didn't want to compete anymore. Miss Dogwood wasn't about winning the crown."

I nodded. It hadn't been. Not for any one of us three.

"I thought about you last June when Sally Ride went up in the shuttle. Did you see that?" asked Dana.

"Yes. Amazing! Remember Miss Vernie told us we'd see a woman fly a rocket?"

"The first female astronaut," Miss Vernie said, shaking her head. "You know, she answered that ad they put in the newspapers that summer of ours." Miss Vernie didn't look any older than I had remembered. But she did walk a little more slowly as we headed down to the pond.

We were quiet for a while, lost in our thoughts as we walked down that shady path I remembered so well. "Can I bring you some plants from our greenhouse at school, Miss Vernie? I've got some that would be real nice in your garden."

"I didn't know the school had a greenhouse," she said.

"No, ma'am, it didn't. Not until I started the garden club." I grinned at her.

She stopped and put her hand on my shoulder. "That's just lovely. How wonderful. I always thought you were good with my plants. And Dana, reading all my magazines. It's no surprise you're going to be a history professor."

"Has anyone heard from Karen?" I asked.

Miss Vernie nodded. "Why, yes. She writes me time and again. She's busy with the drum corps at school. She's the head batonist, you know. Her stepfather goes to all her games."

"People sure can change," I said.

We stepped out of the shady woods into the bright clearing. The pond looked golden that day under the early morning sun.

Dana gazed across the water. "Or sometimes, you're the one who changes. And everything and every person looks different." Then she looked over at me and smiled the biggest, most beautiful smile I'd ever seen.

A thin ribbon of cattails was back around the rim

of the pond. I noticed a man pulling at them. "Who's that?" I asked.

But Miss Vernie's smile told me who it was. "My Charlie came back."

"Did you give him a charm bracelet too?" Dana laughed.

"As a matter of fact, he's got one in his pocket." Miss Vernie clapped her hands and laughed.

"He's never going to get that done by himself," I said.

"I know," she said. "I've just been waiting for him to ask for some help."

"We can help him. Can't we, Dana?"

She took off her jacket and tossed it to the ground. "Absolutely!"

"I'll go get some more shovels," Miss Vernie said.

We rolled up our jeans and waded into the pond. "Cold!" I said, drawing in a sharp breath.

Charlie looked up at us. *"Shh,"* he said. "Look over there." He pointed to the shore.

But it was too late. A turtle, the size of a cereal bowl, slid off the bank into the water.

Dana gasped and then laughed. "I see you've met Earl." She picked up a handful of mud and tossed it at me.

I hurled a hunk of it back at her.

And soon we were sloshing through the muck, our laughs echoing across the pond, skipping above the trees and the water and the flowers, then settling right into the ground next to all the heartache and healing and magic that was all mixed up in there too.